Windsor Heights

Book 1

This book was written for all children everywhere

who have faith—stubborn faith—

and for those who don't,

that they may find it.

— Lisa Long

Windsor Heights

Book 1

Lisa Long

Illustrations by Marian Long

Windsor Heights Books

Windsor Heights – Book 1
By Lisa Long

Copyright © 2004, 2017 by Lisa Long
ISBN: 978-0-9753566-0-9

Published by:
Windsor Heights Books,
Riverside, CA
www.windsorheightsbooks.com

Illustrations by Marian Long

Author's Note:
This story is based on real persons and events. Permission to appear on these pages has been received from all named individuals.

Printed in the United States of America

Contents

ACKNOWLEDGEMENTS

I would like to thank God for inspiring me and for giving me more than I ever dreamed of. I would like to thank my children – Lindsay, Jeffrey and Beau – for without them, this book would not have been possible.

I would also like to thank my mom for graciously accepting the assignment of illustrator. As a child I would always ask her to draw for me— a horse, a flower, anything. This book would not be complete without her drawings.

Chapter 1

Lindsay's Lessons

It happened just last week, but to Lindsay it seemed like a lifetime ago. She was on her way once more to her weekly riding lesson. She had just started taking them and couldn't think of anything else. From her first thought in the morning to the last one at night, it was—*horses*. Lindsay rolled down her window in the gray van and stuck her hands out in the wind to dry her sweaty palms.

"Mom, who do you think I'm going to ride today?"

"I don't know, Lindsay. Why? Who do you want to ride?" asked Lindsay's mom, Lisa.

"Well, I kind of feel like riding Fresno because she doesn't pull very hard on the reins."

Lindsay's hands were dry now, so she pulled them in from the window. She slipped on her black leather riding gloves and gathered her thoughts.

"Mom, I have butterflies again."

"So do I," said Lisa.

The drive to the stables was just as fun for Lisa as riding was for Lindsay. It only took two minutes from Lindsay's house to get to Victoria Avenue, and then from there it was only 10 minutes more straight down Victoria Avenue. As soon as they turned onto Victoria, which ran right through acres and acres of orange groves, Lisa would roll down both windows in their van to smell the orange blossoms in bloom. "Linds, can you smell the orange trees? Is that the greatest scent or what?" asked Lisa.

Victoria Avenue was Lindsay's mother's favorite street in Riverside. It was over 100 years old and was listed as a historical landmark. It had two separate lanes for traffic with a big space in the middle filled with big beautiful trees and plants. There were pepper trees, eucalyptus trees, palm trees and rose bushes one after the other on both sides of each lane. In some places, the trees and bushes were so thick that you couldn't even see the cars on the other side of the road passing by. "I do love this road, Lindsay, don't you?"

"Uh huh," agreed Lindsay. "I know, don't tell me. It was named after Queen Victoria of England and people used to drive their horses and carriages on it a long time ago, right?"

"Exactly," confirmed Lisa.

"Mom, you tell me that every time we get on this road."

"Sorry," Lisa said.

Traveling down Victoria Avenue, Lindsay

began saying the street names out loud as they passed them by: "Van Buren ... Jackson ... Monroe ... Adams ... Jefferson ..."

"The streets are named after the presidents of the United States," Lisa explained. Madison Street came next; that was the street the stables were on. Lindsay took off one of her tall black riding boots just as they turned onto Madison Street. "Lindsay, what are you doing? You do not have time to be doing that."

"My sock is twisted and it's," Lindsay said gritting her teeth, "bugging me!" If there was one thing Lindsay hated more than sweaty hands, it was socks that were twisted or loose in any way. She always made sure her socks were perfectly straight on her toes and that they were pulled up high and tight. Then after her socks were in order, she would very carefully pull on her snug tan riding pants over her socks and then put her boots on last. If any part of her socks or pants got twisted or bunched in any way, she would repeat the whole process.

"Lindsay, you're just going to have to live with it today," exclaimed Lisa, as she pulled into the gravel driveway and parked. Lisa saw Anne walking down to the arena. "Let's hurry, Lindsay. I already see Anne."

Anne was Lindsay's riding instructor. She was unique to say the least! Anne was tall and slender, with blonde hair, and she wore fancy clothes, usually with some kind of horse print on them. She was a very, very busy lady as she had three jobs; schoolteacher by day, horse trainer by afternoon and disc jockey by night. As soon as Anne arrived home from teaching school, she would rush straight to the arena to meet her students—fancy clothes, high heels and all. One other thing that made Anne unique was her voice. It was loud and unmistakable, and she wasn't afraid to use it, not one bit, to tell anyone what to do or how to do it.

Lisa and Lindsay walked through the gate

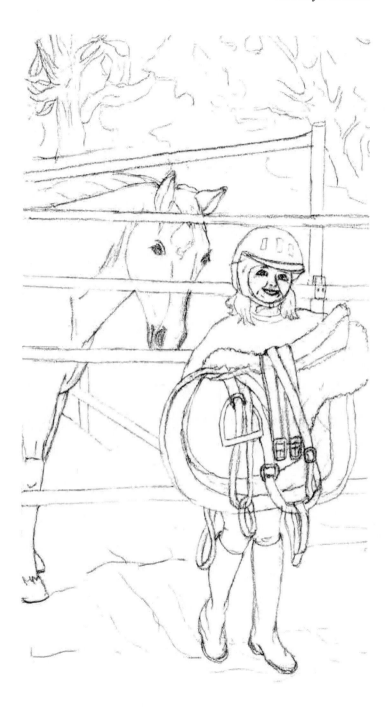

and into the stables. "Hi, guys!" Anne yelled from the arena. "Lindsay will be riding Fresno today, but hurry, you're a few minutes late."

Lindsay excitedly ran to get Fresno's tack out of her locker. Lisa grabbed the small brown English saddle to help, but Lindsay insisted on carrying everything.

"Fresy!" Lindsay called. Fresno was in the far corner of the corral and did not turn around. Fresno was standing ankle deep in mud from a recent rain and looked miserable.

"Go get her," said Lisa. Lindsay looked at her Mom and then stared at the mud for a moment. "Linds, she is obviously not going to come to us, now go get her. She doesn't know us that well yet." Lindsay slid through the rails of the corral, keeping hold of one rail so as not to slip. She carefully made her way around to where Fresno was standing and tossed the lead rope around her neck. Fresno willingly followed Lindsay back through the deep mud to the gate.

Once Fresno was brushed, bridled and saddled, Lisa tried to give Lindsay a leg up into the saddle. "I can do it, Mom, I can get up all by myself," said Lindsay as she squirmed away from her mother. Lindsay lowered one stirrup low enough to get her foot in it, then grabbed the saddle and slowly but surely pulled herself up on top of the horse. "Mom, can you shorten my stirrup now please?"

"Okay, Linds," said Lisa, adjusting the stirrup. "There you go; that's the proper length. Now please be careful; I get so nervous watching your lessons. Oh yeah, do your best because Dad might come with Jeffrey and Beau to watch you."

"Mom, can you hand me my crop?" Lindsay politely asked.

"Where is it?" asked her mother.

Lindsay pointed at the ground near the corral. Lisa handed Lindsay her crop. "Now hurry up," she said.

As Lindsay entered the arena, Anne told her

to begin trotting and catch up to the other riders. "You're looking lovely today Lindsay, and I love your jacket," Anne said. Then shouting to the other students, she called out, "Students, please notice how Lindsay is dressed. That's what I call riding with pride."

It was not unusual for Lindsay to spend an hour getting ready for her lesson, carefully picking out her clothes, sometimes even asking her Mom to curl her hair. At seven years of age, she was Anne's youngest student. It didn't bother Lindsay that she rode with students much older than herself. She was a strong girl, and determined to keep up with the others. Whatever Anne told Lindsay to do, she did it. Lisa would usually sit on the edge of her seat throughout Lindsay's lessons as if she might jump up at any moment and catch her if she were to fall.

"Lindsay, today you will be doing something you have never done before, but trust me, you can do this and so can Fresno." Anne continued,

"First, come over here so I can adjust your stirrups to the correct length. Who adjusted those for you?"

Lindsay looked at her mom and then, without answering, walked Fresno right in front of Anne. "My goodness, I think you have grown an inch since last week. Well, you are going to be tall, no doubt about it. One look at your mom and dad will tell you that. Your mom is taller than me, and I am five-ten. And your dad is way over six feet."

"He's six-foot-five," confirmed Lindsay.

"Well, sweetie, your dad will have to buy you a big horse one day," Anne said as she put Lindsay's foot back in her stirrup. "Everyone, everyone, please ask your horses to stand still so you can pay attention to what I am about to tell you," Anne continued speaking in a loud voice as she walked around the arena using hand movements to add drama to what she was saying. "First, I want you to take your horse over this simple ground pole at

the trot. Then slowly, and I mean slowly, while maintaining the trot, turn completely around and take the series of cross-rails I have set up for you over there." Anne pointed to the cross-rails and continued speaking, "After the last cross-rail, now listen because I don't want anyone to get this wrong. I want you to halt and I mean halt as in stop your horse, don't let him move. Now, who would like to be first?" asked Anne.

Lindsay did not raise her hand. She liked to watch the other riders go first so that she could get a good feel as to how to do it. After all the students completed the exercise, Anne turned to Lindsay, "Lindsay it's your turn, dear."

Lindsay gathered up the reins and squeezed Fresno into the trot, steering her straight at the ground pole.

"Heels down, Lindsay. Keep your eyes up and watch where you're going. Now squeeze, squeeze, Lindsay!" yelled Anne.

Fresno broke down into a walk halfway

through the course. "Try that again, Lindsay, and this time keep kicking. Fresno does not understand what you want if you're not using your legs correctly. And, dear, you have a crop for a reason. Tap her on the rump with it. You won't hurt her and, frankly, she will appreciate a tap of the crop more than a constant kicking of her sides."

Lindsay headed Fresno at the ground pole again. Only this time she really held her legs tight and hit Fresno on the rump with her crop. Fresno went faster and faster. Lindsay started to get off balance, and by the time she finished the course, she could barely get the horse to stop. "Lindsay, sit back and halt. One, two, one, two!" screamed Anne running after Lindsay.

By the time she stopped, she was up on Fresno's neck and in tears. Lisa jumped up out of her seat with a concerned look on her face. "You are okay, sweetie," laughed Anne as she caught up to Lindsay. "Good for you. You kept the trot all the way through the course and you lived through it."

Anne addressed Lisa's concern, "She is fine, really. I wouldn't ask her to do this if I didn't think she could." Lisa took a deep breath and sat back down.

Anne's dogs began barking at the gate. Lindsay's dad was walking up the hill with her two younger brothers, Jeffrey six years old and Beau just three. Lisa liked how handsome and rugged her husband, Jeff, looked in his jeans and newly grown beard. She went to meet them. "Hi, honey," Lisa said to Jeff while hugging both boys at the same time.

"How's her lesson going?" Jeff inquired.

"Well, she nearly fell off a minute ago when she couldn't get Fresno stopped," answered Lisa.

"Is she okay?"

"She was upset for a few seconds, but she's fine now. Her lesson is almost over. Let's go watch the rest," Lisa said. As they walked back to the arena, Anne saw Lindsay's dad and brothers coming.

"Hi, Jeff. Hi, Jeffrey and Beau," Anne shouted in her most polite voice. "Lindsay is doing absolutely fabulous today. She's a good little rider."

It didn't take long for Jeffrey and Beau to get bored. They soon wandered off to their usual spot where they liked to slide down a dirt hill and throw dirt and leaves at each other. They also found it entertaining to throw rocks for Anne's dogs to fetch. "Boys, please do not throw rocks; it scares the horses," yelled Anne from across the arena.

Lisa took the boys to the barn to find something to occupy them. After a short time Jeff walked in saying the lesson was over. "I'll take the boys home and we'll stop and pick something up to eat at the house." Jeff then added, "Hurry up, okay? You guys always take so long to put a horse away."

"Okay, we'll see you at home," Lisa replied.

As soon as Lisa walked out of the barn, there were Lindsay and Fresno walking in with the setting sun shining on them and setting off their every feature. Lindsay's cheeks were a deep pink, her green eyes sparkled and her hair the color of a wheat field was slightly more wavy than usual from blowing in the wind. Fresno's eyes were gleaming like two new copper pennies, her orange fur all wrinkled and damp with sweat. Her nostrils were flared as she was taking deep breaths and beginning to relax. "How did you like your lesson today, Linds?" asked Lisa as she stood there admiring her daughter.

"Great. Fresno is a sweetheart!" Lindsay said as she leaned forward hugging Fresno's neck.

"She really is," agreed Lisa, petting Fresno on her forehead. "All right, let's get her put away now," Lisa added.

Lindsay took both feet out of the stirrups and, while hanging onto the saddle, slowly lowered herself to the ground. Then she took the reins off Fresno's neck and led her into her corral. First, she took off Fresno's bridle, quickly slipped her

halter on and tied her to the corral with the lead rope. Then she removed her saddle, and steam rose up from Fresno's back.

"Mom, can you hand me that brush over there. Anne said she doesn't want to see any saddle marks." Lisa gave Lindsay the brush and helped her put away the tack. Once all of Fresno's fur was neatly brushed, Lindsay ran to get her blanket and threw it in a heap on Fresno's back, diligently pulling and straightening it until it hugged her body perfectly. Lisa reached under Fresno's belly and fastened a hook only to have Lindsay come behind her and unfasten it.

"Lindsay, what are you doing?"

"That's my favorite part, Mom—fastening all the hooks on her blanket." Lindsay proceeded to fasten every one of the hooks all by herself. "Now for the carrot," declared Lindsay as she walked behind her mom and pulled a carrot out of the back pocket of her jeans. Lisa wouldn't dare give Fresno the carrot; she knew that was something Lindsay had to do. Lindsay stroked Fresno's forehead and ran her hands gently over her kind eyes as she munched down every bite of the carrot.

"Okay, Lindsay, can we go now?"

Lindsay got out of the corral and they both began to walk to the van, when suddenly Lindsay turned around and ran back to the corral. Lisa continued walking. After the girl caught back up with her mother, Lisa asked her, "What did you have to do?"

"I forgot to give her a kiss goodnight."

Chapter 2

Driving Home

Driving home, Lisa would usually take a scenic detour through the orange groves, which would give Lindsay enough time to talk about every detail of her lesson.

"Oh, that was the greatest lesson!" sighed Lindsay as she took off her riding helmet, revealing her damp hair stuck to her forehead.

"Lindsay, weren't you scared when you almost fell off?"

"Well, sort of, but you know it really helps when Anne yells, 'One, two, one, two' because then I do it and Fresno just stops."

"What exactly does that mean anyway, 'One, two, one, two'?" Lisa questioned.

"It just means pull on one rein and then the other, back and forth until the horse stops."

Lisa could see Lindsay holding up her hands out of the corner of her eye when she said, "Mom, look."

"I can't right this second. I have to watch where I'm going. Oh, Lindsay! Look at that old farm house set back in the orange groves, isn't it pretty?" Lisa continued, "Now what did you want to show me?"

Lindsay held up her hands again showing her mom how the gloves had made them all black. Lisa raised her eyebrows.

"Mom, Anne said that next week we will be learning how to do emergency dismounts."

"You know, this is what it used to be like

around Grandma's house, before all of the houses you see now were ever built. I think if we ever moved, this would be the area I would like to live in, wouldn't you?" Before letting Lindsay answer, Lisa kept speaking. "I love the orange groves; it makes you feel like you're way out in the country even though you're only a few minutes from town. Can you believe that Orange County used to be like this? It would sure be fun to have enough property to keep horses or even motorcycles, don't you think so, Linds?"

"Mom, you know, I think Fresno is really getting to know me, don't you?"

"Yes, I think so."

"I'm famished!" exclaimed Lindsay.

Lisa looked at Lindsay, not realizing she even knew a word like that. "Dad said he would have food for us when we got home."

"I feel like I could eat ten hamburgers."

It was almost dark when they turned down their street. Lisa could already see their little house with the garage door wide open with Jeffrey and Beau playing inside. As they pulled into the driveway, Bagheera, the family dog, came to greet them as usual. He was an English Mastiff and weighed almost 250 pounds. He had short yellow hair, with a black mask on his face and the kindest soul a dog could have. Bagheera wore a big blue collar with a tag that read "I belong to the Wrights" with an address and phone number. He really didn't need a tag because he never wandered. Lindsay liked to hear her mom say that Bagheera didn't have a wandering bone in his whole body. Anytime Lindsay, Jeffrey and Beau would go outside, Bagheera would go with them and never leave their side. No one ever complained that they didn't keep Bagheera in the back yard because they knew all the children on the block were safer playing because he was there.

The Wrights lived at the end of a cul-de-sac street with quaint little houses, all of which

were of a different design and color. Their house was white stucco with black trim around the windows, a black front door and a black flat tile roof. Because their house was at the end of the street and that's where all the children played, Bagheera's job as guardian was very convenient.

He would lie on the front lawn with his head down between his front legs and look up out of the top of his eyes, keeping watch on the children. If Bagheera became leery of anyone strolling down their block, he would raise his big square head, judge the situation, and sometimes he didn't have to bark or even get up because his looks alone would scare them away.

Lindsay jumped out of the van, patted Bagheera on his head and ran into the garage to play with her brothers, suddenly forgetting about her hunger.

"Lindsay, come on now, you need to get cleaned up so you can eat," reminded her mother.

"Jeffrey, will you please pull off my boots?" asked Lindsay as she sat down holding both legs in the air. Jeffrey was always happy to do anything that would display his strength. Jeffrey was big and strong but had a soft look about him with his creamy complexion, blond curly hair, blue eyes and gentle spirit. With his back to Lindsay and her leg wedged between his legs, he began to pull off one of her tight boots.

"Geez, Lindsay, why do you have to have your boots so tight?" grunted Jeffrey. Lindsay laughed as she used her other foot as leverage on Jeffrey's rear and pushed until her boot came off and Jeffrey fell over on the floor. Bagheera went over and licked Jeffrey in the face, and they all laughed.

"I want to do the next one," chimed Beau.

Lindsay gave Beau her other leg, knowing he was too little to really get the boot off, but she pushed on Beau's rear anyway just to make him laugh. Beau was a sweet and giving boy who found joy in giving toys away to other children on the block, sometimes to the dismay of Lindsay and Jeffrey. He had the same coloring as Lindsay with green eyes and sandy blond hair that waved in the back. Beau was tall for his age and was sometimes mistaken for being one or two years older than he really was.

"Beau, do you want Bubba to do it?" Jeffrey asked. Beau let Jeffrey get the other boot off too, and then they all went inside. Lindsay ran straight to the kitchen with the boys following her. "Lindsay, Dad bought you a hamburger and french fries," Jeffrey said. Lindsay sat down at the kitchen table with her still black hands and dirty face and began to eat.

Jeffrey and Beau sat down, too, even though they had already eaten.

"Lindsay, when you're done eating, do you want to play in your loft?" asked Beau as he sat at the table holding Cheyenne.

"Okay," said Lindsay, "let's bring Cheyenne and Kimba and play animal trainer."

"I'll go get your crop, Lindsay," Jeffrey said as he ran back to find Lindsay's crop in the garage.

Cheyenne was a red longhair Dachshund that also wore an identification tag because she absolutely needed it. Being the scent hound that she was, her nose would often lead her astray. Thanks to her tag and the people who found her, she was always returned. Lisa couldn't count the times the phone would ring and someone would ask, "Do you have a Dachshund?" One lady across their street had their phone number taped to her wall by her phone so she wouldn't have to look at Cheyenne's tag every time she wandered over.

Cheyenne was strategically bought for Beau a year earlier to keep him company when Jeffrey went to school. The plan worked. Beau was constantly occupied with Cheyenne. Wherever Beau was, Cheyenne would be there with him. She did not have much of a choice because Beau kept her on a leash to make sure that she stayed with him at all times.

Kimba was Lindsay's cat that her dad brought home for her when she was two years old. Kimba was not your average cat; she was more like a rag doll. She had long grayish brown hair on top of her head, back and tail and pure white fur like billowing clouds underneath on her tummy and on her legs. She had big green eyes with what looked like black eyeliner around them and a soft pink nose with long white whiskers. She liked to be with the kids and would let them carry her around in any fashion they wished, never clawing or scratching them.

Lindsay finished eating and all three of them ran into her room. Lindsay was the first one up in the loft. "Hand me Kimba, Jeffrey," Lindsay said reaching down over the side of her loft.

"Here, take her quick," grunted Jeffrey while balancing on the ladder and lifting Kimba into the air. Lindsay grabbed Kimba and pulled her into the loft.

"Okay, now Cheyenne," Lindsay dictated.

Jeffrey turned to Beau who was holding Cheyenne. "Give her to me!" he said.

"I can do it!" Beau said.

"No you can't, Beau, you might drop her!" said Jeffrey rather loudly.

"No, I won't!" insisted Beau.

"Yes, you will. Now give her to me!" demanded Jeffrey as he grabbed Cheyenne from Beau's arm and hoisted her up into the loft. After Cheyenne and Kimba were safely up in the loft, Jeffrey climbed up.

"Beau, don't forget the crop," reminded Lindsay. Beau grabbed the crop and started up the ladder.

Once they were all in the loft, they began their favorite game: Animal Trainer. Since Beau already had the crop and didn't want to give it up, he was 'Trainer' first. There really weren't

"KIMBA"

any rules; it was just a make-believe game. Each acted as if he were a lion trainer in the circus, pointing the crop first at Kimba, then at Cheyenne. Kimba liked being in the loft but didn't really care for Cheyenne so she stayed on the opposite side of the area. When Lindsay got her turn, it was as though she really believed she was in the circus, like she truly was a lion trainer, and the boys were mesmerized by her enthusiasm. Sometimes Beau would not play at all. He would be content to sit quietly and watch Lindsay and Jeffrey play as though he was watching them on television.

"Lindsay, Jeffrey, Beau," called Lisa.

"What?" they chorused.

"It's getting late, so I would like for all of you to get your pajamas on and brush your teeth."

"Can we play for just a little longer?" asked Lindsay.

"Do you guys have Cheyenne up there?" Lisa asked in concern.

"Yes," they all said together under their breath.

"You know that I don't like for you to have her up there; it's dangerous. If she were to fall, she would get hurt. Now let me have her." Lisa climbed halfway up the ladder and pulled Cheyenne to safety. "Actually, all of you come down right now, please, and do as I asked."

Beau climbed down the ladder first and started into his room. Lisa was in the boy's room looking through their books. "Mom, can Cheyenne sleep with me?" Beau humbly asked.

"Beau, have you done what I asked yet?" Lisa asked in return as she continued searching for a bedtime story to read to the children. "How about *Balto, the Bravest Dog Ever?*" suggested Lisa loud enough for Lindsay and Jeffrey to hear although they were in different rooms.

"Mom, you always cry when you read that book," shouted Lindsay from her room.

"Well, I won't this time," insisted Lisa.

"Come on, Beau, Mommy will help you brush your teeth.

Lisa walked with Beau into the bathroom, and with the boy in front of her, she cradled his head in her left arm and held it firmly in place almost like a headlock. With her other hand, she began to vigorously brush his teeth. Lisa heard something in the hallway, and when she looked to see what it was. There was Jeff standing shaking his head and laughing to himself.

"What?" asked Lisa.

"I have never in my life seen someone brush their kid's teeth the way you do it." Jeff continued, "Do you want me to help you put the kids to bed?"

"No, that's okay. I'm going to read them a story and then I'll come to bed."

As soon as everyone had their teeth brushed and pajamas on, they all huddled into the boys' double bed that they shared. "Scoot over, Jeffrey," demanded Lindsay.

"Lindsay, you scoot over," Jeffrey said back to her.

"Everybody is squishing me," said Beau.

"Okay, now is everyone comfortable?" Lisa asked. And she began to read. *This is a true story about a very brave dog. His name is Balto. The year was 1925. Balto lived in Nome, Alaska. Balto was a sled dog. One cold winter day, a terrible thing happened in Nome. Two children got very sick.*

Lisa continued reading, but when she got to the part of Balto delivering medicine through a blizzard to save the children, her eyes welled up with tears and she stopped reading for a second to let the tears drain back down her tear ducts. Lindsay and Jeffrey looked up at their mom and smiled. "I'm not crying," Lisa said.

"Well, your eyes are all red," said Jeffrey matter-of-factly.

"Keep reading, Mom," said Beau.

All over America people cheered for Balto.
They read about his bravery in the newspaper.
Balto was the most famous dog in the world.

"That's the end of the story. Goodnight."

"Mom, can I sleep with Cheyenne?" Beau asked.

"Okay, I'll go get her," said Lisa as she tucked Jeffrey and Beau snug in their bed. Lisa found Cheyenne in the garage and brought her into the boys' room. The boys had already moved over onto each side of their beds, leaving just enough room for Cheyenne to be wedged between them.

"Mom, say our prayers," reminded Jeffrey. Lisa said their prayers and then went into Lindsay's room to tuck her in.

"Goodnight, Lindsay, you've had a big day," Lisa said as she tucked Lindsay in, making sure to pull the covers up straight and tight just the way she liked them.

"Mom, will you say my prayers, too?"

"Okay, what would you like to pray about?"

Lindsay started in with her prayer requests. "Fresno, Bagheera, Cheyenne, Kimba. Oh yeah, speaking of Kimba, can I sleep with her?"

"I guess," said Lisa exasperated. Lisa went to find Kimba and brought her back and tucked her in with Lindsay. "Are you ready to pray now?" Lisa asked.

"Yep," said Lindsay as she stroked Kimba under her chin just the way she liked it.

"All right, close your eyes, Lindsay."

Lindsay shut her eyes tight and held her hand over Kimba's eyes. "Dear Lord, thank you for this day, thank you for my family and all of my animals. Thank you for Fresno, Bagheera, Cheyenne and Kimba. Please keep them safe. Thank you for this house, my room, my bed and all of my toys. Amen."

Lisa gave Lindsay a kiss goodnight, hoping the prayer was adequate so she wouldn't have to start all over again.

"Mom, are we going to Grandma's tomorrow?"

"Yes, we are. Goodnight, Lindsay."

Chapter 3

The Concrete Donkey

It was a beautiful spring morning – the kind when mockingbirds sit outside your window and sing until you wake up. Lisa was still in bed when she heard Jeff talking to the children, saying, "Dad has to go to work today, but Mom will be taking you to Grandma and Grandpa's. Be good and have fun. I'll be home by the time you get home."

"Bye, Dad," the children chorused.

Lisa heard the front door close and ran out to catch Jeff before he left. "Bye, honey, I'll see you later." Jeff walked back to the front door where Lisa was standing in her pajamas. He wrapped his arms around her and gave her a kiss goodbye.

"You're beautiful in the morning, you know that?" Jeff said starting back to his truck and then added, "Call me on my car phone if you need me for anything."

By the time Lisa got herself in the van, all three kids plus Cheyenne were there waiting patiently for her. "Well, I guess it won't hurt to take Cheyenne with us today," Lisa said, as she saw Beau holding her in the back seat. Lisa started the van, turned on the radio to their local country station and started down the road. Within one minute it happened.

"Mom, I'm thirsty," a voice came from the back.

"Lindsay, can you please take care of Beau while I'm driving?" asked her mother. Lindsay confidently pulled a water bottle out of her bag and handed it to Beau.

"Oh, I love this song. You guys, this is Randy Travis!" Lisa turned up the radio and began singing. *Yeah I'm gonna love you forever, forever and ever amen, na na na na na na na ....* The kids giggled and held their hands over their ears.

Once they arrived at Grandma's, Lisa no sooner parked the van than Lindsay jumped out and ran over to the concrete donkey that was sitting in Grandma's front lawn for decoration. Lindsay straddled the donkey pretending to ride it when all of a sudden the whole donkey fell over because one of its legs was broken.

Lisa ran over to Lindsay, who sat crying on the ground holding her foot. "Lindsay, what in the world happened? Come on, let's get you up," Lisa said, minimizing her pain. Lindsay tried to stand up and then fell down again crying even harder. "Let me see your foot, Lindsay. Shhh, you'll be all right," her mother assured. Lisa took Lindsay's sandal off and then proceeded to take off her sock, revealing her black and blue bruised foot.

Lisa carried Lindsay into the house and lay her down on the couch in the family room. Just then Grandma came walking in from one of her back bedrooms. Grandma had long, thick and shiny dark brown hair which lay in big curls halfway down her back. She had bright blue eyes and an endearing smile. "Well, I thought I heard someone in here," Grandma said in a sweet voice. Grandma lived in such a big long house that it was hard to hear things from one side to the other.

"Hi, Mom," Lisa said. Just then Jeffrey and Beau came running through the hallway with their arms extended ready to hug Grandma.

"Well, how are you?" she asked the boys, while hugging both of them. Grandma then saw Lindsay on the couch and looked at Lisa as if asking for an explanation.

"The donkey fell over and landed on Lindsay's

foot. I think I might have to take her to the hospital."

"Oh, dear, that thing. Let me get her some ice to put on it," Grandma said.

"I'm still riding in my lesson this week!" insisted Lindsay as she tried to catch her breath. "No matter what!"

"Lindsay, if you can't walk, you're not going to be able to ride," Lisa said in a calm manner.

"Yes, I will, I don't care what the doctors say," yelled Lindsay in distress.

After about a half an hour of resting with ice on her foot, Lisa had Lindsay try to see if she could put any weight on it. "Lindsay, let's see if you can stand now," Lisa said.

Lindsay agreed to try, and when she did, it only started her back to crying.

"Hi, Grandpa, Hi, Grandpa!" the boys said excitedly. Grandpa had just walked in the front door.

"Who's that I hear crying?" Grandpa asked.

Jeffrey and Beau told Grandpa the whole story while he was still standing in the entry. "Well, that's too bad. Maybe this will make her feel better." Grandpa held up three small brown paper bags. "One for you, and one for you, and one for Lindsay," he said. Jeffrey and Beau each looked inside their bag and saw an assortment of candy. "I hope your Mom won't mind, but I knew you were coming over today and I wanted to get you each a little something," said Grandpa.

Beau grabbed the bag for Lindsay and ran into the other room to give it to her. "Lindsay, Lindsay, look what Grandpa got you. Candy!"

Lindsay stopped crying long enough to look in the bag and then closed it again. "Lindsay, don't you want a sucker? It's cherry, your favorite!" coaxed Beau, trying to make her feel better.

"Well, Lindsay, the boys told me what happened. Can I take a look at your foot?"

asked Grandpa as he walked in the family room. Lindsay nodded. Grandpa delicately lifted her leg and examined her blue and purple foot.

Grandma and Grandpa watched the boys while Lisa took Lindsay to Chapman Hospital. They had to go to the emergency room because that was the only part of the hospital that was seeing patients at that time. The entire time they waited to see the doctor, all Lindsay was concerned with was being able to ride in next week's lesson. "Mom, I don't care if my foot is broken, I am riding and that's final," Lindsay said, looking a mess with red eyes, red cheeks and dirty clothes.

Lisa told Lindsay, "We'll just have to wait and see what the doctor says. Now please quit getting so upset about your lesson."

"Lindsay Wright," called a nurse. Lisa picked Lindsay up and carried her into a back room. "Can you tell me what happened, young lady?"

asked the nurse, looking at Lindsay.

Lindsay began welling up with tears again as she tried to tell the story. "I was at my Grandma's house ... and there was this donkey ... and it ... fell over and landed on my foot." By then Lindsay was sobbing.

"Okay, sweetheart, let's get an X-ray and see what's going on in there," the nurse said, patting Lindsay on the leg.

After Lindsay's foot was X-rayed, the doctor came in and reviewed the pictures. "There doesn't appear to be any broken bones," the doctor said scratching his chin while looking at the X-rays. "But most definitely there is some damage to the cartilage which doesn't show up on an X-ray."

"What does that mean? Can she walk on it?" Lisa asked.

"Have her stay off it a day or two, elevate it for swelling and ice it twice a day for the next two days," the doctor ordered. "She should be up and around in no time," he said to Lisa. "Now stay away from those donkeys," the doctor said, smiling at Lindsay. Lindsay smiled.

When they got back to Grandma and Grandpa's, Grandma and the boys were just sitting down for lunch. "Is her foot broken?" Jeffrey asked.

"No, no bones are broken, but the doctor said that she has damaged cartilage," Lisa explained. Lisa carried Lindsay to a chair at the table and sat her down.

"We're having haystacks for lunch," chirped Beau as he tied Cheyenne's leash to one leg of his chair. A haystack was a pile of crunched-up chips, shredded chicken, lettuce, tomato, cheese, olives and sour cream piled high on your plate.

"Lindsay, I'm sorry about your foot. I'll have to fix that donkey," said Grandma as she set a haystack in front of Lindsay. Grandma laughed as the kids immediately began picking tomatoes and olives out of their haystacks.

"Lindsay, after you eat, don't you want to

have your sucker?" asked Beau as he set the brown bag right in front of her plate.

"I'll have it if you don't want it," said Jeffrey.

"I do want it," Lindsay said.

Grandma looked at Lisa and Lindsay sitting side by side and said, "I sure think you're going to look like your mommy one day, Lindsay." Lindsay looked at her Mom and smiled.

When the kids had finished eating, Lisa dunked a napkin in her water glass and one by one held the kids as she wiped food off their face. "Mom, can you carry me to the piano?" Lindsay asked.

"Okay, let's go," Lisa said as she picked Lindsay up and carried her in the living room. In the corner of the room that had a view of all of Orange County sat a big, white, grand piano. Now huffing and puffing, Lisa plopped Lindsay down on the piano bench. Because Grandma's house was so spacious, it was very tempting for the kids to run around. Even Lisa got the urge to rough house a little.

"Hey, boys!" called Lisa as she lay down on her back in the middle of the room putting both of her feet in the air. "Do you want to do airplane?" Jeffrey ran in first and she put her feet right in the middle of his stomach and holding onto his hands, pushed him as high as she could stretch her legs then let go of his hands so that he was balancing on her feet all by himself.

"My turn, my turn," shouted Beau. Lisa did the same to Beau who was stiff with fear.

"Relax, I won't drop you," assured Lisa as she laughed.

"My turn again," said Jeffrey. Grandma came into the living room to see what all the commotion was about. "Watch, Grandma!" he said excitedly as Lisa repeated the trick. Grandma laughed. "The way you mother those children reminds me of the same way a lioness mothers her cubs."

"What exactly does that mean, Mom?" asked Lisa, as she now had Beau balancing on her feet.

Grandma explained, "Oh, just the way you grab them and clean their faces and the way you tumble them around so roughly."

"Mom, my foot hurts," Lindsay said somberly still sitting at the piano but not playing.

"Okay, boys, that's it. We need to get Lindsay home now. Tell Grandma goodbye."

"Can't we stay a little longer?" pleaded Jeffrey.

"Your sister doesn't feel well. Now please both of you boys gather up your belongings and go get in the van," insisted Lisa.

Beau ran back to the kitchen realizing that he had left Cheyenne tied to his chair.

Grandma walked them out to their van while Lisa carried Lindsay. "Grandpa and I will come visit you next time, okay?" Grandma told the children as if to make things better. "Sorry you got hurt today, Lindsay." Before they even got off Grandma's street, Lindsay started in, "Mom, I am still riding Fresno this week, right?"

"Lindsay, it really doesn't look like it right now,

but let's just see how you feel in a few days."

"Well, I am," Lindsay said as she lay her head back on the seat and closed her eyes to keep the sun out of them.

"Lindsay, do you really think you're going to be able to get your tight boots on over that swollen foot?" asked Lisa. "Lindsay … Lindsay …"

Lindsay had fallen asleep. Lisa looked in her rearview mirror. Jeffrey, Beau and Cheyenne were asleep, too.

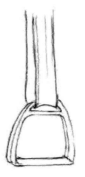

Chapter 4

Emergency Dismount

Lindsay could overhear her mom and dad discussing her lesson in their bedroom. She hobbled down the hallway and pressed her ear to their door. "Just let her try it I guess, and if she can't handle it, then bring her home," she heard her dad say.

"Well, I think her foot hurts more than she's letting on. But she has been insisting that she ride all week. You know, I admire her bravery," she heard her mom say. "I'll go tell her she can go."

Lindsay limped to her room as quickly as she could and sat on her bed pretending to read a book.

"Lindsay, Dad said you can go. But if your foot hurts too much, I want you to tell me, all right?"

"I will, but the doctor said stay off of it for a few days, and that was a whole week ago," said Lindsay.

"Lindsay, don't tell me how long it's been; I know how long it's been," scolded Lisa. "Now you best get ready, I want to get there a little earlier today." Lindsay immediately began her ritual of getting on her riding apparel.

After what seemed like a longer time than usual for Lindsay to get ready, Lisa went to check on her progress. There was Lindsay struggling with her left boot trying to force her foot into it. "Lindsay, you're not going to get your foot in that boot with the bandage still on it." Lisa bent down and took off the bandage. Lindsay grimaced as she yanked on her boot.

"I don't know about this," Lisa said in a concerned voice.

"I'll be fine, Mom. Besides, it feels kind of good with my boot on." Lindsay put on her helmet and gloves. "Mom, do you know where my crop is?"

"The last time I saw it, it was in your loft," answered Lisa. Lindsay limped toward her ladder. "Here, Linds, I'll get it for you." Lisa started up the ladder and could see the crop on the other side of the loft out of her reach. As she crawled all the way up in the loft, she hit her head on the ceiling. "Ouch!" Lisa exclaimed as she rubbed her head.

Lindsay laughed. "That happens all the time," she said still laughing.

"Lindsay, I don't think it's funny. Next time don't leave your crop up there."

Lisa and Lindsay were the first ones at the stable. They took their time walking through the stable, admiring all the different horses. "That one is Cooper, Mom. His show name is Coup De Ville. He's Anne's jumper."

Cooper was a big gray Thoroughbred that always had his head stuck way out in the aisle of the barn to get attention. Lisa broke off a piece of Fresno's carrot and gave it to Cooper. "Mom, what exactly do you think you're doing?"

"What does it look like I'm doing?" Lisa asked sarcastically.

"It looks like you are giving Fresno's carrot to another horse!" Lindsay said as she grabbed the rest of the carrot out of her mother's hand.

"He sure is my kind of horse, big and tall. I wonder if Anne would let me ride him," pondered Lisa.

"I don't know, but I am going to see Fresno," said Lindsay. She walked to Fresno's locker, pulled out her saddle, bridle, and grooming kit and left the rest of the carrot in there for safe keeping. When Lindsay walked up to Fresno's corral, the horse still did not face her, but as

Lindsay hung the saddle on the corral and prepared to go in and get her, Fresno couldn't help but turn her head around to see what was going on. "Hi, Fresy, come on, do you want to ride?" coaxed Lindsay.

"That's right, Lindsay, talk to her and see if she'll come to you today," encouraged Lisa.

"Come on, Fresy!" Lindsay said in a soft voice.

Suddenly, the silence was broken. Lisa could hear Anne in the stable. "Well, hello, Cooper, how's my big luv doing? Oh, hi, guys. Great, you're here early today. Lisa, I need to talk to you about a few things, like, right now, because I really need to get down to the arena."

"Yeah?" Lisa asked.

"Okay, there's a show coming up in a couple of months that would be great for Lindsay. She could go in the walk-trot class and do very well with Fresno, so think about that. And also, Fresno's owner would like to do a partial lease on her, and I really think you should do it. She wants $50 a month, and Lindsay can ride her any day but Saturday, which is when her owner rides. She will also let you take her to shows. Think about it because, if you did lease her, Lindsay would be guaranteed Fresno every week. Believe me, it's a good deal and Fresno is worth it," concluded Anne, turning to walk away.

"Wait, Anne, I wanted to let you know that Lindsay hurt her foot pretty badly last week. You see, this donkey, not a real one but a concrete statue, fell on her foot, and she had to have X-rays and everything. Well, anyway, I thought maybe you could be easy on her today," requested Lisa taking notice that Anne didn't seem to be paying any attention.

"Oh, I see. Now I really do need to get to the arena," Anne said walking off in a delicate fashion so as not to get her nice shoes dirty.

Lisa turned her attention back on Lindsay, "How's Fresno doing? Do you need any help?"

"Mom, did you see her come up to me all by herself? I just need help tightening her girth and can we go to that show?"

"I hope so."

Lindsay began walking Fresno down to the arena and then stopped and turned back to her Mom. "Mom, are we going to lease Fresno?"

"We'll see, but right now you need to concentrate on your lesson."

Lindsay was the first rider in the arena and began walking Fresno around to warm her up. By then, Anne had changed into her riding boots, but she still had on her fancy clothes. She was preparing the arena for her lesson by placing poles on the ground just the right distance apart. "Anne, my Mom wants to know if she can ride Cooper," Lindsay blurted out. Lisa sank into her chair.

"Well, Cooper is quite a horse and frankly, I don't think your Mom could handle him. You can begin a posting trot now," Anne said with a smile on her face. "Lindsay, did you know that Fresno is an ex-racehorse?"

"She is?" Lindsay said excitedly.

"Great," mumbled Lisa under her breath.

"Lindsay, you are posting way too high. Posting is a flick of the hips, not jumping out of the saddle. Feel the rhythm, Lindsay, up … down … up … down, that's better," Anne said. Anne had each student begin a posting trot as they entered the arena. Lindsay and Fresno were now warmed up, and Fresno was acting like she wanted to run. Suddenly Fresno began leaping and jumping, sometimes with all four feet off the ground. Lindsay struggled to stay in control as she stood in her stirrups with a tight grip on the reins. Lisa stood up and put both hands over her mouth. Anne quickly reacted to the situation running over closer to where Lindsay was, yelling all the while. "Sit back, whoa, whoa! One, two, one, two. Pull harder, Lindsay, and stop her *now!*" Fresno finally settled down and

Lindsay gathered herself. "Okay," Anne said getting her breath, "What Fresno just did with you, sweetheart, was nothing that you can't control, and now Fresno knows that as well. I just want you to remember to keep your seat next time. You have greater control when you remain in the saddle. But you did great just to stay on her. Now then, let's get her back on the rail and pick up the trot again." Lisa sat back down with a knot in her stomach. Anne yelled up to where Lisa was sitting, "Lindsay can control this horse; you just saw her do it. And Fresno was not being mean, she just feels good, especially with the weather being a little cooler than usual."

Lisa nodded.

"All right, students, listen up! Just as I told you last week, we will be learning how to do something that could quite possibly save your life one day if your horse was ever out of control and headed for danger. This something is called an emergency dismount."

Lisa stood up to remind Anne about Lindsay's foot, "Excuse me, Anne, I really—"

Anne didn't hear her and went right on speaking. "There is another reason that I like to teach this, and that is to get you over any fear of falling that you might have. First, I will perform one correctly for you."

Anne borrowed a horse from one of her students and first displayed an emergency dismount at the halt, then got back on and proceeded to trot right down the middle of the arena. While trotting and shouting out instructions, she vaulted off her horse and rolled onto her back. She stood up with dirt all over her and, while dusting herself off, said, "There, now, did you see how I rolled onto my back? That is to absorb shock, and notice how I still have one rein in my hand. Anne proudly displayed the one rein she still had a hold of. I must say that was a brilliant dismount, and I would like for all of you to try it one at a time.

Lindsay didn't like the looks of the demonstration and took Fresno to the back of the line. "Sarah, why don't you be first?" said Anne. "And please start trotting at the first pole and vault off before you get to the second pole."

Sarah had been taking lessons from Anne for several years and did not want to do the exercise.

"Come on, Sarah, you've done this before," encouraged Anne.

"Oh, Anne, I hate this. You know I hate this," complained Sarah as she walked her horse to the starting point.

Anne began instructing Sarah, "Start trotting ... good ... and get ready ... and vault! Vault, Sarah. Now!"

Sarah did the emergency dismount, but she lost her horse. All the students began to laugh, which eased the tension. Anne walked over to Sarah's horse and led her back to Sarah still sitting in the dirt.

"Next time, Sarah, you really need to keep hold of one rein," Anne said using Sarah's mistake as an example of what not to do. "Remember people," Anne yelled, "you are responsible for your horse, so you must keep hold of one rein as you jump off. And now for Lindsay," said Anne. "Sweetie, bring Fresno up to the starting pole and take her in a nice slow trot." Lindsay did just that, except for the nice and slow part. "Slow her down, Lindsay, slow her down now!" shouted Anne.

Fresno passed the second pole, and Lindsay never dismounted. By the time she stopped, she was at the end of the arena. "Bring her back around and let's try it again," yelled Anne. Again, Lindsay was ready for Anne's command at the first pole. "When I say vault, that's when you jump off, just exactly like I showed you." Lindsay gathered her reins. "Start trotting … that's right … right now, Lindsay … vault!" Lindsay passed the second pole, and Anne continued to yell, "Vault! Vault!"

Lindsay was almost to the end of the arena with Fresno trotting very fast when, out of desperation, she jumped off and landed on her back on an end pole of the arena. Fresno stopped the minute Lindsay jumped off and didn't move a muscle. Lindsay began to cry, and Anne went over to help her.

"Now, you're not hurt are you? See, honey, you did it and look; you still have her rein in your hand. Good girl. Next time jump off right when I tell you to so you won't end up with your head out of the arena like it is now."

Anne helped Lindsay to her feet, dusted her off and helped her back on Fresno. "Do you want to try that again?" Lindsay shook her head no.

"Students, please begin walking your horses until they are cooled out. That will conclude our lesson for today." Anne quickly left the arena.

As Anne was walking out of the arena, Lisa got her attention. "Anne, you know I think it is a good idea for us to lease Fresno. After all, she is

Dismount

Lindsay's favorite horse to ride. Can you please let her owner know."

"Yes, I will and I think you made the right decision," Anne replied with a smile.

"Anne, would it be okay if I rode her as well?" asked Lisa hopefully.

Anne took a moment to respond. "You know Fresno is really not that big of a horse, and she is twenty-seven years old. No offense, but you really are much too big for her."

"Oh, yeah, absolutely, I didn't really think about that," said a humiliated Lisa.

"I'll call you to confirm the lease agreement," Anne said as she continued on her way. Lisa waited until Lindsay had Fresno in her corral to tell her the good news. "Lindsay, I told Anne that we would lease Fresno. I hope Dad won't mind, but if we weren't the ones to lease her, someone else would. Then you would really never get to ride her in your lessons again. Leasing Fresno will kind of be like owning her. You won't have to worry about who you will ride anymore."

Lindsay beamed with happiness. She ran to get the carrot out of the locker. Lindsay spoke softly to Fresno as she gave her the broken carrot, "Did you hear that, Fresno? We're going to lease you." Fresno shut her eyes halfway as Lindsay stroked her cheeks. "Mom, I think Fresno is glad."

Lindsay limped out of the corral. "You had quite a lesson today. Are you okay after that fall? It looked like it hurt your back," Lisa said.

"My back and foot hurt right now."

"You look like you've been in a war," Lisa said looking at Lindsay limping with dirt smudged all over her face.

"I feel like I've been in a war."

"I think a hot bath will make you feel better."

"That's exactly what I was thinking," said Lindsay.

As they walked back through the stable on their way out, there was Cooper asking for one last pet. Lisa stopped to pet him. "Lindsay, don't let anyone fool you. I could handle him just fine."

Lindsay smiled.

Chapter 5

Practice Makes Perfect

"Mom, can we go to the stables today after church?" Lindsay asked.

"We'll see."

"I want to practice my dressage test. I think I have the whole thing memorized now," said Lindsay proudly.

"I'm sure you do, with as many times as you have drawn it on paper and practiced it on your bike, I can't see how you could forget it," said Lisa.

After church, Lisa and Lindsay did end up going to the stables. Jeffrey and Beau didn't want to go and stayed home with their dad.

As Lisa and Lindsay walked through the stable, Lindsay began to holler out for Fresno. "Fresy! Fresy! We're coming!"

"Lindsay, I don't think she can hear you from here."

"Yes, she can, Mom. She knows me now," Lindsay said continuing to call her. "Fresy, I brought you a carrot."

Lisa was surprised to see Fresno stick her head out of her corral. "Lindsay, you're absolutely right; she does know you now. Gosh, remember when she didn't want anything to do with us?"

"See her, Mom? She's looking for me."

When Lindsay reached Fresno's corral, Fresno dropped her head down to the level of Lindsay's head and nickered to say hello.

"Well, hello to you, too," Lindsay said as she immediately slid herself through the rails of the corral and began unfastening the buckles on her blanket.

Fresno turned her head around to see what Lindsay was doing. She stretched her neck as far as she could to reach Lindsay's head. Lindsay giggled as Fresno smelled her hair with her big nostrils. "I'm going to keep using that strawberry shampoo, Mom. Fresno loves it."

"I can see that," Lisa said getting in the corral too.

"Mom, I can do this by myself."

"I know, but I want to help." Fresno sighed as Lisa and Lindsay worked her over with all the different brushes in the grooming box. Lisa picked up the curry comb to use on Fresno next.

"Mom, Anne said not to use that brush because the metal is too harsh and it dulls their coat."

"Oh, you learn something new everyday. Maybe that's why Indian was never that shiny. I never did have a single lesson all the time I had

horses," said Lisa as she tossed the curry comb back in the box.

"How long did you have Indian for, Mom?"

"Well, let me think for a second. Okay, I got Daisy when I was six years old. Then, when I was around eight, we got Indian, and my Mom sold him when I was around twelve. So I had him about four years."

"Why did Grandma sell him?"

"I really don't know. I guess I just lost interest."

"Well, I'm never losing interest, and I'm never ever going to quit riding, not in my whole entire life," pledged Lindsay.

"I sure hope not. Now, let's get her saddle on," Lisa said as she pulled the saddle off the top rail of the corral.

Lisa walked beside Lindsay and Fresno down to the arena. The sun was just peeking through the late morning fog, and the birds were beginning to sing. Lisa pulled up a chair and sat down with the sun facing her. "Lindsay, just warm her up at the walk for a little while," Lisa said while thawing out in the sun. Anne's house was set on the side of a hill, and from the arena you could look out over a whole grove of orange trees. "Lindsay, look." Lisa pointed to where you could usually see the orange groves. The fog was thick and just settling down on the grove, revealing just the tops of the trees. "It looks like bushes growing in the clouds."

Lindsay admired the view for a moment. "Oh, that looks neat. Can I start trotting now?" Lindsay asked, changing the subject.

"Go ahead."

It wasn't long before Lindsay wanted to practice the dressage test that she would be doing in the upcoming show. "Mom, I'm going to try my test now. Just tell me if I make a mistake."

Lisa reached in her jacket pocket and pulled out a piece of paper with dressage instructions on it.

Lindsay took Fresno out of the arena and

turned her around. "Tell me when to start," said Lindsay.

"Okay, go," Lisa told her. Lindsay trotted Fresno confidently into the arena which had certain letters placed in the corners and along the sides to help the rider perform written tests. Lisa read the test aloud as Lindsay rode. "Enter at A working trot rising... at C track left... at E circle left twenty meters... at E straight ahead to C... at C develop medium walk... you're doing good, Lindsay, but the judges will be judging your circles and how nice and round they are."

She continued through her test, not making a single mistake as far as memorization. "That's great, Lindsay, you really do have an amazing memory. Anne will be so pleased that you know the test."

"I want to try it again," Lindsay said. She practiced the test again, and again, and again.

"Lindsay, I think that's enough for now. Let's get her put away."

Lindsay reluctantly agreed and lowered herself down from Fresno's back. As Lindsay's mother watched her unsaddle Fresno, she asked, "Lindsay, don't you ever wish you could ride bareback?"

Lindsay looked at her mom, "You mean with no saddle?"

"Yeah, you really get a good feel for the horse that way and when the horse starts sweating, it makes you stick to their back. Maybe I can teach you one day."

"Thanks, but no thanks. I think I'll stick with my saddle," insisted Lindsay.

Grandma decided to come and watch Lindsay's next lesson. "This is Lindsay's last lesson before the show," Lisa told Grandma. Lindsay proudly showed Grandma how Fresno knew her and how she could put the bridle and saddle on all by herself.

"Wow, Lindsay, you have really been learning about horses, haven't you?" Grandma said.

"Mm hmm," agreed Lindsay as she brushed the tangles out of Fresno's tail.

"I hope all of my four o'clock students are almost ready," Anne yelled out as she walked through the row of corrals.

Lisa got Anne's attention, "Anne, I would like for you to meet my mom, Marian." Anne reached to shake Grandma's hand. "Hi, I'm Anne, Lindsay's trainer. Lindsay is a good kid, and a good rider."

"Oh, well, thank you," said Grandma. "How long have you been a trainer?"

"Do you know, I have been training horses for thirty years, ever since I was twenty years old. I actually even trained horses as a teenager as well, but officially since twenty. And this week I'm turning fifty. Can you believe it? And for a birthday present to myself, I am giving myself a facelift! I know, it sounds crazy but I want one, so I have been saving money for the past couple years for it because

I knew that I would eventually get one. Now I can afford it and frankly, I deserve it," Anne said smiling.

Grandma smiled at Anne and said, "You look good. I wouldn't think you would need a facelift."

"Well, after the divorce and all, I just want a little something for myself, you know."

"Sure," agreed Grandma.

"Well, nice meeting you, and I hope you can make it to the show," Anne told Grandma.

"Yes, we will be there," Grandma said.

"Students, I will be in the arena, so please finish up whatever it is you are doing and then please come right down," Anne said as she turned and walked away.

"She sure isn't shy, is she?" Grandma said.

"No, she sure isn't," agreed Lisa.

Lindsay was still fighting the knots in Fresno's tail. "Lindsay, that's enough now. You need to get to the arena," Lisa said. Lindsay led Fresno out of the corral and then confidently climbed aboard.

"Boy, Lindsay, you sure are strong to get up on her all by yourself," said Grandma. Lindsay smiled and trotted off to her lesson.

As Lisa and Grandma walked to the arena, Lisa forewarned Grandma, "Look, Mom, Anne is very passionate about her lessons, so don't let it bother you if she starts yelling or anything. She tells it like it is, good or bad."

"Oh, all right." Grandma said laughing.

"Lindsay, please keep Fresno farther behind the horse in front of you. If the horse in front of you kicks Fresno in the face, it will be no one's fault but yours. And I'm sure Fresno's owner would not appreciate it," scolded Anne.

Lindsay slowed Fresno down and let the horse in front of her get farther out in front.

"That's right, good girl. Sarah, you need to tighten your reins. That's it. Now everyone is looking pretty much in control at this very moment. One more time around and then come into the center of the arena," Anne said.

One by one the students rode into the center of the arena and stopped in front of Anne. "How lovely. Okay, now then, students, every one of you needs to go over your test today so you will be prepared for the show this weekend. I hope all of you have it memorized. Who would like to try it first?" Anne asked. No one raised their hand. "Those of you who have the test memorized, please raise your hand." Still no one raised their hand.

Lisa stood up and yelled, "Anne, Lindsay knows her test."

"Oh, well, why didn't you say something? Lindsay, would you please perform the test for the sake of the other, much older students who have not yet memorized their test."

Lindsay took Fresno out of the arena and asked Anne to tell her when to start. She rose to the occasion and rode a mistake-free test.

"Bravo!" said Anne. "Students, that is exactly what all of you need to learn. Lindsay, you will do very well at the show, mark my words. Thank you, Lindsay."

When the lesson was over, Anne had a word with the students. "People, every one of you needs to be here Saturday to bathe and clip your horses. Make sure all of your show clothes are clean and in a garment bag ready to go. You don't want to be looking for things at the last minute. If you're riding with me, I'll be leaving here and I mean leaving at five a.m. sharp! Lindsay, I'll be trailering Fresno and you are riding with your family. Does any one have any questions? Well then, if you have any questions later, you can call me with them. I am sure we will have a very fun day."

Saturday couldn't have come soon enough. Lindsay had never given a horse a bath and was anxious to learn. "Mom, I'm going to suds up every single hair on Fresno's body," Lindsay said as she waited for her Mom to find the shampoo in Fresno's locker. "She is going to be the prettiest horse at the whole show when I get done washing her. I'm going to put conditioner on her, and then I'm going to braid her mane and tail," Lindsay said proudly.

"Ahah, found it," Lisa said as she pulled a bottle of shampoo out of the locker. Before Lisa could even turn around, Lindsay had grabbed it and made a dash to the wash rack where Fresno was waiting patiently for her bath. She turned on the hose and started to wet Fresno's legs; then she squirted her sides with the cold water and Fresno sucked up her belly and threw her head up. "Lindsay, slow down. Let her legs get used to the temperature of the water before you start on her sides," cautioned Lisa. Once Fresno was completely wet, Lindsay got the shampoo bottle and squirted a big blob of shampoo on Fresno's back and then another on her tail. Lisa washed her mane and Lindsay washed her tail.

Some other riders were bringing their horses into the wash area. "Hi, going to the show?" Lindsay chirped while still lathering up Fresno's tail, which now was so thick with suds that Lindsay had it dripping off her elbows. Lisa laughed to herself at Lindsay's enthusiasm.

"Lindsay, not everyone is going to the show, you know."

"Can I rinse her off now?" Lindsay asked.

"Go ahead," said Lisa.

Lindsay got the conditioner and repeated the whole process. "Mom, you have to feel Fresno's tail. It's so soft."

"Yes, it is soft; now let's get her dried off and finish up."

Fresno gleamed as the warm sun dried her. Lindsay braided her tail and slipped it into a tail bag to keep it clean. The blanket was next, and Lisa made sure to let Lindsay fasten every hook. "Okay, Lindsay, back she goes. She's all done."

Lindsay was a mess and seemed to like it that way. She proudly walked Fresno back to her corral. "Fresno, please, pretty please, don't roll. I'll see you tomorrow at the show," said Lindsay.

"Come on, Lindsay, let's go," called Lisa.

Lindsay ran over to her mom and noticed that she was laughing. "What are you laughing at?"

Lisa pointed to Fresno rolling in the dirt creating a nice cloud of dust.

"Fresno!" yelled Lindsay.

"She'll be fine; we can brush her at the show. Let's go home now," Lisa said.

Chapter 6

The Show

When they arrived at the entrance to the show grounds, there was already a line of trucks and trailers waiting for their turn to enter.

As soon as they pulled into the show grounds, Anne spotted them. She motioned for them to park where she was standing. After they parked, Anne gave them the okay sign. "Hi, guys! I've already picked up Lindsay's show packet. It has her cross-country test and penny in it. Just have her wear the penny over her coat and make sure that you tie it down nice and flat so the judges can read her number. I would highly suggest that you have Fresno tacked up and ready to go by eight-thirty. That will give Lindsay plenty of time to get her warmed up. After her dressage test, I'll walk the cross-country course with her."

"Thanks, Anne," said Lisa.

"No problem, I'll see you in a bit," Anne said.

Jeff chuckled after Anne left, "I tell you what, she is one of a kind."

"Lindsay, do you want to go say hi to Fresno?" Lisa asked.

"Need you ask?" Lindsay said as she reached for her shoes.

"Honey, do you want to go?" asked Lisa.

"Not right now, I'm going to set up the canopy," Jeff said.

Lisa and Lindsay walked over to Anne's trailer. Fresno perked her ears up and turned her head when she heard Lindsay's voice. "Hi, Fresy, are you ready for the show? I'll bring you an apple later. Gosh, Mom, I thought she would be dirty after she rolled on the ground but she's not."

"I know; she looks great. Let's go look at the other horses," Lisa suggested. They continued walking down the row of trailers, admiring all the different show horses.

"Mom, look at that pony. Isn't it cute?"

"Look at that one, Linds, he is gorgeous." They kept walking until they came to the dressage arena where some of the more advanced riders were taking their test. "Lindsay, notice how that lady is making her circles? Nice and round."

Lindsay nodded her head in acknowledgement.

Now, sounding more like a coach, Lisa said, "I know it's harder than it looks, but I want you to remember that, and try for nice round circles."

"Oh, my stomach is in knots," moaned Lindsay as she rubbed her stomach.

"Maybe this isn't a good idea to watch. How about we get some hot chocolate?" Lisa suggested.

"Good idea," Lindsay said.

While sipping hot chocolate, they slowly walked back to the motor home. Lindsay noticed other girls putting on their show coats, hair nets and polishing their boots. "Can I start getting ready when we get back?" Lindsay asked.

"I don't see why not," Lisa said. Then pointing she added, "Hey, Lindsay, look who I see!" Lindsay finished the last bit of her hot chocolate, threw her cup in the trash and ran as fast as she could to them.

"Granny! Papa!" she called. Papa held out his arms to catch her as she ran to him. He picked her up and gave her a kiss on her cheek.

"How's my number one grandgirl?" he asked. Lindsay liked it when he picked her up. She liked his big arms and silver beard and hair. And most of all she liked it when he called her his number one grandgirl. Lindsay was his first grandchild, so he told her that he would always call her that.

"Hi, Granny," Lindsay said, still in Papa's arms.

"Hi, sweetheart," Granny said as she leaned over and gave her a kiss. "Oh, I am so excited to see you ride Fresno today!" said Granny, smiling with a twinkle in her soft blue eyes.

Lisa caught up with them, "Hi, Pam, Hi, Elmer." Granny and Papa were Jeff's mom and dad.

"And there's my number one daughter-in-law," said Papa as he hugged her. Lisa gave Granny a hug too.

"Where's Fresno? Can we go see her?" Granny asked.

"Sure, she's right over there," Lisa said, pointing directly at Fresno.

Lindsay started walking with Granny and Papa. "Linds, I thought you wanted to get ready, remember?"

"Oh, yeah," Lindsay said, turning around.

Lindsay didn't waste any time putting on her

show clothes, including a black velvet helmet cover.

"Oh, Lindsay, you look like such a little proper rider with your black boots, black gloves, black coat and hat! Turn around and I'll put your hair in the net."

"Mom, why do we have to wear nets in a show?"

"I don't know. I guess the judges don't want to see anything flopping around," Lisa said as she tucked Lindsay's ponytail into the net. Lindsay grabbed a towel and began wiping her boots with it.

"What are you doing?" Lisa asked.

"Polishing my boots. I saw some other girls doing it, and I want my boots to be just as shiny as theirs," said Lindsay proudly.

Lisa grabbed her camera and said, "Smile. Lindsay. Oh, you look so proper!"

Lisa brushed Fresno one last time, then placed the fluffy, white, freshly washed pad on her back and nestled the newly oiled saddle down onto it and cinched her up with the freshly washed girth. Today, everything would be perfect and clean and exactly in place. Next, Lisa put the bridle on Fresno, making sure not to hit her teeth or her eyes. She straightened down all the straps and fixed Fresno's mane and forelock, making sure every hair was where it should be. "Lindsay, she's ready. Let me help you on her today so you won't get dirty or anything."

Lindsay let her Mom help her on. "Take her over to the warm up arena," directed Lisa. "Anne is over there with her other students right now."

"Bring Fresno in, sweetie, and begin walking her. That's right. My, you both look lovely," Anne said. Lindsay walked Fresno around and around all the while keeping an eye on all the other riders. Some girls had green coats; others were wearing blue. Some horses had their manes braided in little tiny braids all the way down their neck. Some horses had a French braid at

the very top of their tail, and other tails had been cut straight off at the very bottom to make them look thick and shiny.

Lisa videotaped Lindsay as she warmed up Fresno. "Lindsay, come here," Lisa called. Lindsay turned Fresno around and brought her over to the rail where her mom was standing. Lisa spoke to Lindsay in a quiet voice, "Lindsay, you and Fresno are the best team out there. Just try to relax and have fun. I know you will do great."

"Lindsay, you should be trotting Fresno now," called Anne.

"I have to go," Lindsay told her mom as she immediately followed Anne's instruction.

"Okay, Lindsay, let's get your heels down a little more, hands down, that's right, shorten your reins and sit up straight. Yes, nice posting trot! That's it! Beautiful! H – X – F, change rein, good girl. Change your diagonal."

Lindsay sat in the saddle for two beats instead

of just one to change her diagonal. "Remember, Lindsay, rise and fall with the shoulder on the wall."

Lindsay looked down at Fresno's outside front leg and made sure she was sitting in the saddle when that leg was down.

"You can walk now. Remember, heels down, correct diagonal and round circles. When they call your number, take Fresno over to the gate and wait for them to ring the bell. After the bell rings, that means you have one minute to begin your test. You're going to do just fine," Anne said confidently. "And remember to salute the judge when you are finished, exactly as I taught you. Show me your salute." Lindsay put her reins in her left hand, dropped her right hand down to her thigh and bowed her head.

"Perfect!" exclaimed Anne.

"Lindsay!" someone called. Lindsay looked over to where her mom was standing, and there were her mom and dad, Grandma and Grandpa,

Granny and Papa and Uncle David and Aunt Judy, all waving and holding their cameras, ready for her to ride. Lindsay smiled and took Fresno over to greet them. "Gee, Lindsay, you look great out there. I didn't know that Fresno was so pretty," said Aunt Judy. Lindsay stretched her arm behind her and patted Fresno on her rump.

"Good luck, Lindsay!" said Uncle David.

"Thanks," said Lindsay.

"Lindsay, they called your number," said Lisa, trying to conceal her nervousness.

"I know," Lindsay said as she turned Fresno around. Lindsay confidently took Fresno to the starting gate where she waited for the rider before her to finish her test.

"Oh, my stomach is in knots," Lisa told Judy.

The judge rang a small bell indicating that they were ready for the next rider to enter. Lindsay entered the arena and stood Fresno at A and waited for them to ring the bell again.

The bell rang again, and Lindsay began her first dressage test in her first show. Lisa videotaped every second while talking to herself, "That's it … okay, now circle … slow down … okay, get ready … don't forget, don't forget … salute." Lindsay came out of the arena with a smile on her face. Anne was there to greet her.

"You did fabulous!" exclaimed Anne. "That is the best she's done!" she added proudly to Lindsay's whole family.

"Lindsay, you did it! You didn't forget anything and your circles were really nice. I'm very proud of you!" Lisa said.

"Mom, there were tracks in the arena left from the other horses and I just followed them when I did my circles," Lindsay exclaimed.

Everyone laughed and walked back to the motor home to wait for the cross-country portion of the show. "I am so glad that we got to see her ride," Judy told Lisa. "You know, I knew she would do well, but I didn't know she would be that good. She's a natural. She was the best rider in her class. I'll bet she takes first," declared Judy.

Just after Judy said that, Jeff came walking over from the judges' booth and said, "They just posted the scores, and Lindsay is in first place!"

"See. I knew it," Judy said matter-of-factly.

"If she has a clear round cross-country, she will keep first, but if she has one refusal, she could lose it," explained Lisa.

As Lindsay's ride time drew near for cross-country, she prepared herself again by putting her black jacket on. Granny was brushing Fresno and Grandma was cleaning her face with a wet rag. When Lindsay went outside to get on Fresno, Anne was there.

"Oh, Lindsay, you don't have to wear your coat for cross-country. Do you have a polo shirt?" asked Anne.

Lisa stepped up behind Lindsay, "No, she doesn't have a polo shirt. I didn't know she would need one," said Lisa, slightly irritated.

Lindsay did look hot in her black jacket. She looked around at the other girls getting ready for their cross-country ride. Everyone had changed out of their formal coats and put on colorful clothing like racehorse jockeys wear. There were colors everywhere, the brighter the better. "Well, she'll be fine in her coat," Anne said walking off.

"You know, that upsets me! This is our first show. How am I supposed to know what to bring?" Lisa said. Then she added, "Sorry, Lindsay, I didn't know you needed anything else."

Lindsay took Fresno back to the warm-up arena and began jumping her over the cross rails. Back and forth Lindsay went. Fresno began to look a little tired. "Lindsay!" shouted Lisa.

Lindsay trotted Fresno over to her Mom.

"What?" asked Lindsay.

"I think you are wearing Fresno out. Maybe you better let her rest before they call your number," Lisa said.

"Number fifty-one, Lindsay Wright and Fresno, will you please come to the starting gate?" said a voice over the loud speaker.

"This is it, Lindsay. Good luck!" said Lisa. Lindsay stood Fresno in the starting gate and waited for her turn. She had walked the course earlier with Anne and had to memorize eight jumps. Lisa had her video camera ready to capture her first jump. Lindsay took Fresno out of the starting gate at a slow trot and headed her to the first small jump, no bigger than a foot high. Fresno stopped. She was just too tired. Lindsay turned her around, and this time, trotting faster, Fresno jumped the jump and went on to jump every other jump in the field. It was a nice round, but the first jump cost Lindsay first place.

When the show was over, all the riders stood around and waited for the ribbons to be handed out. Over the loudspeaker came, "And fifth place goes to Lindsay Wright!" Everyone clapped as Lindsay walked up to accept her very first ribbon. It was a big, pink ribbon that said Fallbrook Horse Show–Fifth Place. Lindsay's Dad picked her up and gave her a kiss. Lisa took a picture of them. It had been a wonderful day.

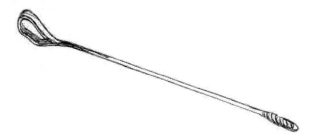

Chapter 7

The Unexpected Wish

In the months that followed the show, Lindsay continued her weekly lessons on Fresno. She enjoyed Fresno as much as always and was sometimes able to see her on weekends.

Lindsay's lessons seemed to be lacking a point lately though. There wouldn't be another show for months, and Lisa wondered how they could keep up with the cost of weekly lessons. The bills added up quickly, so it was getting harder and harder to afford them.

One morning over breakfast Jeff and Lisa began discussing this issue. "Football has a season, baseball has a season, basketball has a season," Jeff stressed. Then he added, "Riding never stops. It just keeps going every week, every year."

"I guess," Lisa figured.

"Well, Lindsay is going to have to stop at least for a little while. You know there are other things this family needs, and these riding bills are killing me."

"I know; maybe she can take the summer off," Lisa suggested.

"Yeah, for sure. I mean I hate to pull her out, but things are just a little tight right now," Jeff said, trying to justify his decision.

"I agree. Don't worry. I'll tell her," Lisa said.

On their way to the stable one day, Lisa decided to tell Lindsay what her Dad and she had decided. "Lindsay, come June, we are going to have to pull you out of lessons for the summer," said Lisa in a serious tone.

"What? Mom, I don't want to be pulled out of lessons!"

"I know. Not right now. I said in June and that's in a couple of months. Just for the summer."

"Mom, that's not fair."

"Lindsay, that's just the way it's going to have to be for a while. You know lessons aren't cheap! And we spent a lot of money on the show."

As they pulled into the gravel driveway, Lindsay forgot all about their conversation and jumped out of the van. Lindsay was an old pro around the stables these days. She knew every horse and every person by name and knew where everything was. Fresno was always happy to see Lindsay and would always walk right to the fence and hang her head over the gate and nicker when she saw her coming. Lindsay could saddle and bridle her on her own and even get the girth plenty tight around Fresno's belly all by herself. She had been taking lessons consistently for over a year on the same horse and had developed a bond with Fresno. They each seemed to know what the other was thinking and feeling.

"Mom, can you lengthen my stirrups one notch, please? They feel too short," asked Lindsay as she took both feet out of her stirrups.

"You sure are growing fast, Linds," Lisa said, adjusting her stirrup leathers.

"Oh, guys, please stop what you're doing," yelled Anne, walking briskly through the stable. "Lindsay, get down, sweetie. I have different plans for you today. You'll be riding with a bare back pad," Anne said as she unbuckled Fresno's girth and slid the saddle off Fresno's back. Anne handed the saddle to Lindsay. "Take this back to the locker and get the blue fuzzy pad," directed Anne with a look on her face that said trust me.

Lindsay did just as Anne said and came running back with a flimsy blue fuzzy pad. "You want me to ride in this?" asked Lindsay with a funny look on her face.

"Yes, I most certainly do and it will be good for you. I should have had you riding in a pad sooner than this. Now let's see it," Anne said holding out her hand. Lindsay handed the foreign object over to Anne. Anne placed the pad on Fresno and buckled the strap under her tummy. "Okay, come on. I'll give you a leg up," Anne said.

"I don't know about this," hesitated Lindsay. "What about stirrups? Where do I put my feet?"

"Lindsay, that's how I used to ride all the time. It's very comfortable because your legs just hang down," assured Lisa.

"Okay, but if I fall off …," Lindsay said as Anne helped her up.

"There, you see, you are fine. Now please walk Fresno to the arena, and I will be there in a minute." Lindsay began walking Fresno as Anne had said, and a slight smile was beginning to develop out of one corner of her mouth.

"You like it, don't you?" Lisa insisted, laughing.

"Well, it does feel kind of good," admitted Lindsay.

The blue fuzzy pad opened up a whole new world of riding to Lindsay. She couldn't be quiet about it. "That was the greatest lesson of my life!" she exclaimed as she buckled her seat belt for the ride home.

Lisa laughed as she started the van for the ride home, "Lindsay, you say that after every lesson! You even say that when you have fallen in a lesson."

"I know, but that was so cool. I want to ride with a bare back pad next week!"

"Well, I don't think Anne wants you using a pad every week. But I knew you would like it after you got used to it," Lisa said.

"Oh, man, my legs felt so good. And I didn't have to hear Anne yelling, 'Keep your heels down!'" Lindsay said as she laid her head back on the seat.

"Speaking of Anne yelling, are you okay with that? I mean, are you happy with her as a trainer? Because if you're not, I need to know," Lisa said in a serious tone.

"You know, she does yell, but I know what she wants, and it doesn't bother me. I like Anne as a trainer because she takes riding serious, and so do I!" Lindsay said in a manner that defied her age.

"Okay, just checking," Lisa said.

"Mom, can I take my ribbon for share tomorrow?" asked Lindsay.

"For goodness sake, no! Linds, you've already brought that for share at least two or three times. I'm sure that you have something your friends would want to see besides your pink ribbon again, don't you?"

"I guess so," sighed Lindsay.

Just as they were approaching their street, Lisa pulled over and stopped. "Lindsay, I see Cheyenne over there in those bushes."

"Where?"

"Over there; watch she'll come out in a second ... see her! Can you go get her? She has no business being all the way down here." Lindsay got out, and trekked across someone's front lawn and plucked Cheyenne out of their bushes.

As Lindsay got back in the van with Cheyenne, Lisa scolded her, "Cheyenne, what are you doing! Don't you know you can get lost!"

Lindsay hugged Cheyenne to save her from her mother's wrath. "Do you think she knows she's in trouble, Lindsay? Look at the way she's hanging her long nose straight down," Lisa said.

"Well, Dad says her brain is probably the size of a pea," Lindsay said, and they both began to laugh.

When they got home, the boys were out

playing on the block with Bagheera. "Boys, you have to put Cheyenne away if you're not going to watch her," Lisa said, getting out of the van, holding Cheyenne up for evidence. The days were getting longer now and the block was full of activity. There were kids roller blading, biking, jumping rope and playing hopscotch.

"Mom, can I play?" Lindsay asked, already sitting on her bike.

"Go ahead, but not for long. We'll be having dinner soon."

Later, after dinner Lisa sent the children to their rooms to get dressed for bed while she cleaned up the kitchen. When she went to check on the kids, Lindsay was sitting on her floor in her pajamas playing with Kimba. "Mom, look." She held Kimba up, displaying the baby dress she had put on her.

"Very cute, Lindsay," Lisa said as she turned to leave.

"Mom, wait."

"What?" asked Lisa.

Lindsay was silent for a moment.

"What?" Lisa asked again.

"I want a horse," Lindsay spit out. Lisa walked over and sat down on the edge of Lindsay's bed.

"What did you say?"

"I want a horse of my own."

"Lindsay, I can't believe my own ears. I thought you loved Fresno."

"I do, I do, but she's not mine, and I really want a horse of my own, a black horse," Lindsay clarified.

"But Fresno is like your own and you even ride her more than her owner," Lisa said, still in shock.

"I know, but I really want a black horse," Lindsay said adamantly.

"Why black? That doesn't seem like your type. Have you really thought this out? I mean,

why not a palomino? I used to always want a palomino. You know, blonde hair, blonde horse," suggested Lisa, making light of Lindsay's serious request.

"Mom, don't try to talk me into a yellow horse. You already tried to make purple be my favorite color when red has always been my favorite color. And black is my favorite color horse," Lindsay said, making her point clear.

"Okay, fine, Lindsay, black can be your favorite color horse. But we don't have horse property, and I am not going to board a horse."

"Mom, *if*, and I mean *if*, I do ever get a black horse, I'm going to name him Midnight."

"Lindsay, *if*, and I mean *if*, you ever did get a black horse, I'm sure that it would already have a name, and I am not going to change a horse's name. And I am not going to get a baby black horse just to name it Midnight! That's a pretty tall order, and I really can't do anything about it. You know I would love to have a horse, too, and the boys always talk about having a motorcycle, but you know we don't have the space here. Do you realize that, in order for us to buy you a horse, we would actually have to buy a house!"

"Mom, my other favorite names were Rainbow Chaser and Lickidy Split, but my first choice is Midnight," Lindsay said as though she didn't hear a word her mother had just said.

Lisa gave Lindsay a hug and said, "There's only one thing that I can tell you, Linds."

"What?" Lindsay asked, all ears.

"Pray about it. Have you already prayed about it?" Lindsay shook her head no. "Well, that's the only thing I know of that can help you. Pray about it every day," Lisa said.

Satisfied with that, Lindsay smiled and wrapped Kimba up in a blanket. She grabbed her crop and took her into the boys' room, and asked, "Do you guys want to play animal trainer?"

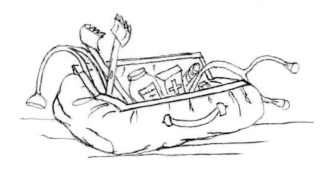

Chapter 8

Cheyenne's Secret

Lindsay seemed to accept her time off from riding well, filling up her time playing with her brothers and friends on the block. Even though the summer was over and Lindsay was back in school, she was not back to her riding lessons. And she made sure that her parents were aware of it.

"Lunch time!" announced Lisa one hot Saturday afternoon. Lindsay, Jeffrey and Beau came in from playing one after the other with Bagheera and Cheyenne following right behind.

"My goodness, all of you have pink cheeks! I think after lunch you guys need to settle down. Maybe you can color or something," Lisa said. "Beau, what's that in your hand?"

"It's a lizard!" Jeffrey answered for Beau.

"Did he catch it or did you?" Lisa asked.

"He did, Mom. I saw him; he just snuck up on it and then covered it with one hand and grabbed it with the other." Beau smiled and nodded in agreement while petting his lizard on the nose.

"Beau Justin, I didn't know you knew how to catch a lizard! I'm very proud of you. Now can you please set it free for a little while?" Beau shook his head no. "I'll bet your lizard would like to eat lunch too. Beau, if you set him free, then he will be able to eat lunch, too. And that will make him happy," explained Lisa.

"Here, Beau, give me the lizard and I'll put it out," Jeffrey said.

"No, I'll do it!" Beau snapped and took the lizard out.

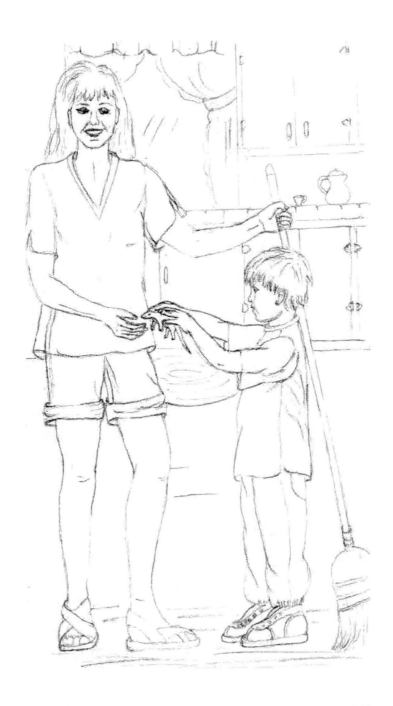

After lunch, Lisa gave the kids some blank white paper and crayons. Beau was in the rainbow stage of coloring and colored every inch of his paper in different colors until there was not a stitch of white left showing. Jeffrey drew an airplane.

Lindsay drew her specialty—a horse. "Jeffrey, pass me a black crayon," Lindsay said.

Jeffrey was so busy coloring that he handed Lindsay the whole box of crayons without even looking up. Lindsay found the black crayon and started in on the horse.

"Lindsay, that sure is a nice horse you've got going there. I guess that's not Fresno is it?" commented Lisa.

"Nope, it's Midnight!" Lindsay said matter-of-factly.

"Oh yeah, that's right, your dream horse."

"Mom, when do I get to start lessons again? I thought you said I could when school starts back and that was last month," reminded Lindsay.

"That was the plan, but things are just so busy. And now the holidays are right around the corner. I really think it would be best for the whole family if you waited until January or February before we put you back in lessons," Lisa explained.

"But, Mom, you said—" Lindsay started.

"Lindsay, I won't have you talking back to me. I know exactly what I said, and sometimes things change. I'm just not sure right now exactly when you will start lessons again," Lisa said.

"But, Mom, I am dying to have a lesson," cried Lindsay.

"I know, and you will. You're just going to have to be patient," Lisa said.

Beau had completed his picture and was on his way out of the kitchen when he stopped to pick up Cheyenne, who was napping on the kitchen floor. Cheyenne would usually sleep in an out-of-the-way spot like a closet or behind the couch but today, like the past couple of days, she would sleep anywhere she could. "Beau, don't pick her up. She's tired," Lisa said.

"Mom, you keep saying that. What's wrong with Cheyenne anyway? All she does is sleep nowadays," Lindsay said while putting the finishing touches on her drawing.

"I don't quite know. I think I will have Dr. Vered come and see her," Lisa said.

That night when Jeff got home from work, Lisa had a private conversation with him. "Honey, I need to talk to you about something," Lisa said.

"What?" Jeff asked. "And why are you being so secretive?"

"Look, Cheyenne is acting funny lately. Sleeping a lot, a little irritable, just weird, you know?" Lisa explained.

"And …?" Jeff said.

"I think she's pregnant," Lisa blurted out.

"What?"

"I don't want the kids to know until I find out for sure. You know, I don't want them to be excited and then get let down if I'm wrong about this," Lisa said.

"This can't be happening! I mean, I thought we were going to have her bred when she was three years old to a purebred Dachshund and then sell her puppies for $500 each. Isn't she too young? She's only a year," Jeff said, freaking out. Lisa started laughing. "Oh, great, and you think this is funny? Give Dad some puppies. That's all I need. This isn't happening," insisted Jeff.

"Well, we'll see after Dr. Vered looks at her," assured Lisa.

"You know, I knew it wasn't right letting your dog just run around the block. You know I wasn't raised to let dogs run free," Jeff said slightly irritated.

"She's been out plenty of times when I had nothing to do with it," Lisa said, settling the score.

"Fine, just get Doc Vered out here to see her

as soon as possible. How much is that going to cost? This is just great! You know they say a purebred dog can be ruined by having mutts," Jeff said.

Lisa laughed again at Jeff's way of thinking. "Honey, think about it! That's not true. Cheyenne won't be ruined. Maybe she's not even pregnant. Maybe she's sick. Even if she did have mutts, we could always have her bred later to a purebred."

"Okay, I can't talk about this anymore. Just call Doc," Jeff said, exasperated. Then he added in a self-comforting tone of voice, "Doc and I get along great; he'll tell me everything is fine."

Doctor Vered agreed to see Cheyenne later that same day. Lindsay, Jeffrey and Beau watched out the window for his big mobile vet to come rolling down their street. "Here he comes, here he comes!" the children shouted as they ran out the front door to greet him. Bagheera followed, wagging his tail. The side of his vet truck had a sign that read 'Born Free' with pictures of all kinds of animals, large and small, wild and tame. "Hi, Doctor Vered!" the children said.

"Hi," the doctor said to the children as he gave Bagheera a pet on the head. "So something is wrong with Cheyenne, I hear," he said in his somewhat quiet voice. Doctor Vered was a compassionate man who loved all animals, and the animals knew it. He was rather small in stature with dark curly hair and glasses, which made him look more like a scientist than a doctor. "Well, where is she?" the doctor asked walking in the already-open front door. Jeff greeted the doctor in the entryway.

"Hey, Doc, good to see you! Come on in," Jeff said, even though he was already in.

"Cheyenne is sleeping in my room now," Lindsay said, directing the doctor to her room. Doctor Vered kneeled down beside Cheyenne.

"Hi, girl. How are you feeling?" Cheyenne wagged her tail but didn't get up or even lift her head. "Well, she seems happy," the doctor said as he stroked her body and pushed on her belly to check for pain.

"Do you know what's wrong with her, Doctor?" Lisa asked, concerned. The children sat quietly waiting for an answer. Jeff and Lisa stood quietly in the doorway.

"Well, I've definitely seen this behavior before."

"You have?" asked Lisa.

"Yes, I have," he said, putting his stethoscope away. "It is my opinion, especially due to the fullness that I felt in her abdomen during my exam, that she is going to have puppies."

"Puppies?" exclaimed Lindsay.

"There is nothing to worry about, I assure you. Just let her rest as much as she wants and give her plenty of good food. I would say her puppies might be born towards the end of December."

Jeff couldn't keep quiet any longer, "Wait a minute, Doc. I mean, Doc, are you sure? You know, maybe she's just sick or something."

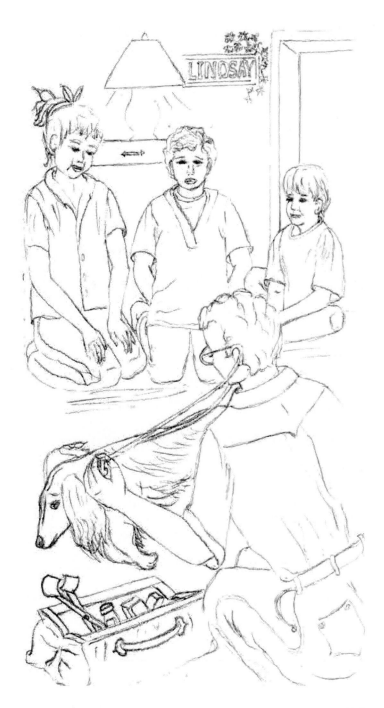

Doctor Vered looked up at Jeff with a rather certain look on his face and said, "Oh, yes, I'm sure that Cheyenne is only pregnant."

"Oh man! I don't think I can handle this," Jeff said.

"Well, don't worry. Cheyenne can handle it just fine," assured Doctor Vered as he closed his bag.

Lindsay, Jeffrey and Beau began to run around the house shouting, "Cheyenne is having puppies; Cheyenne is having puppies! Yippee! Yippee!"

"Thank you for coming out so soon, Doctor," said Lisa, walking him to the door.

"Oh, sure, just call me if you have any questions," he said. Before Doctor Vered left, he briefly turned his attention toward Bagheera, remembering a previous injury. "How is Bagheera's hind leg treating him lately?" he asked as he ran both of his hands down Bagheera's back leg.

"He gets around pretty good, but he does

have trouble getting up now and then," answered Lisa.

"It won't hurt to give him an aspirin a day," advised the doctor, walking out the door.

"Okay, Doctor, thanks again," Lisa said. Lindsay, Jeffrey and Beau ran to the front door with smiles a mile wide and told the doctor goodbye.

Chapter 9

Christmas Puppies

"Mom, can we keep one of Cheyenne's puppies?" Lindsay asked while stirring Cheyenne's dinner in a bowl.

"I doubt it; I think Bagheera, Cheyenne and Kimba are enough for us," Lisa said.

Lindsay loved making special recipes for Cheyenne. She placed a dog vitamin in the bowl and stirred it in. "I'm calling this 'Lindsay's famous doggie delight.'" She said as she put the bowl in the microwave oven to warm it up just the way Cheyenne liked it.

"What exactly is in that dinner?" asked Lisa.

"Left-over chicken, one egg, one piece of bread, a little cheese and a little oil," Lindsay stated proudly.

Cheyenne sat on the floor waiting patiently for her dinner. She was growing bigger every day, and now, when she would sit down, her back legs would spread apart and her stomach would touch the ground. Lindsay set the bowl down in front of Cheyenne and then sat down beside her to watch her eat. "I wonder how many babies she's going to have," Lindsay pondered.

"I know she will have at least four because I felt them. And I am not so sure that she won't have six," stated Lisa.

Jeffrey and Beau came into the kitchen and sat down beside Cheyenne to watch her eat with Lindsay. Beau began to ask his daily questions, "When is Cheyenne going to have her babies? Can she have them in my room?"

"Beau, quit asking when Cheyenne is going to have her babies. It's bugging me!" demanded Jeffrey.

"Beau, I guess she could have them any day now. I just don't know exactly. Only Cheyenne knows," Lisa answered.

Beau smiled and petted Cheyenne, who finished her bowl of food and then waddled into the family room and laid down under the Christmas tree.

"Mom, Cheyenne looks funny when she walks now, and her belly is only like an inch off the ground," observed Jeffrey.

"Wouldn't that be cool if Cheyenne had her babies under the Christmas tree on Christmas morning," Lindsay said.

"Yeah, and we each got to keep a puppy for Christmas!" Beau said.

"I think all of you are deliriously tired right now and need to go to bed," Lisa said, bursting their bubble.

That night after the kids went to bed, Jeff and Lisa stayed up and watched a movie with a fire burning in the fireplace. Christmas was only a few days away now, and Cheyenne was huge. Her favorite thing to do was to sleep in front of the warm, crackling fire. Jeff took notice of Cheyenne and showing a sliver of compassion asked, "Is Cheyenne going to be alright? She looks way too big—like she's going to pop!"

"I don't know. I was thinking the same thing myself," said Lisa.

"Why don't you call Doc and ask him?"

"Yeah, I think I will. Honey, you know I'm just as excited as the kids are for her to have her babies. I don't care if she decides to have them at midnight; I'm going to be up with her and help her."

Jeff laughed, "There's no way that you can stay up till midnight. Anyway, dogs don't need help delivering babies. Doc said they can handle the whole thing on their own."

"Did I tell you that I think she might have six puppies?" Lisa said.

"Six? Why six? How do you know?" Jeff asked.

"Well, when she lies real still, I can feel them. It feels like she has three sausages in a row on each side of her stomach," explained Lisa.

"Did you have to say that?" Jeff said with a bad look on his face; then he mimicked Lisa, "Three sausages in a row." Lisa laughed.

The next night Lisa and Jeff stayed up late wrapping Christmas presents in the garage. Lisa began to shiver, "Honey, I don't feel good. I feel like I'm coming down with the flu."

Jeff put his hand on her forehead and exclaimed, "You're burning up! Why don't you go to bed and I'll finish this."

Cheyenne greeted Lisa on her way to bed. Her tongue was hanging out of her mouth. "Cheyenne, what are you doing?"

Cheyenne just looked up at her with her

eyes all big and began panting and then started running around the house. Lisa sat down in her room with Cheyenne and tried to calm her. "What's wrong?" Cheyenne, still panting, ran out of the room and then ran back in, now panting even more heavily. "Oh, Cheyenne, you are going to have your babies," Lisa said still shivering. "Why now? Not when I'm sick, Cheyenne."

Lisa could not console Cheyenne. Nothing helped. Cheyenne was restless and ran from room to room with her long pink tongue hanging clear out of her mouth. She kept running to the side of the boys' bed, so Lisa picked her up and put her on the foot of their bed. She finally got quiet and laid her head down.

Lisa patted Cheyenne on her head, "Cheyenne, I don't know what to do for you. But I'm so sick, I need to go to bed," she said with her body shivering and teeth clattering.

Lisa went back out to the garage. "I thought

you were going to bed," Jeff said.

"I was, but then Cheyenne started running around. I think she's going to have her puppies."

"Are you going to stay up?" Jeff asked, while putting a big red bow on a box.

"I want to, but I am so tired. I f-f-f-feel awful. She's on the boys' bed right now."

"Great. Where is she going to have them?" Jeff asked.

"I have no idea. But there's nothing else I can do. I feel so bad. I wanted to be with her when she had her babies, but I am just so s-s-sick right now. I need to go bed. Good night," Lisa said.

That night, Lisa tossed and turned sick with the flu. Around midnight she got up to get a drink of water and went to check on Cheyenne in the boys' room to see if she was still on the bed. Cheyenne had jumped off the bed, and had given birth to two puppies right there on the floor next to the boys' bed.

Cheyenne was relaxed and nursing the two beautiful chocolate brown pups. Lisa sat down beside her and talked very quietly to Cheyenne so as not to wake the boys, "Cheyenne, you did it. You did it all by yourself, and they are beautiful. They are no bigger than my hand, Chey-Chey."

Cheyenne sat up and delivered her third pup right in front of Lisa. "I knew you had more than two in there."

The third puppy just lay on the ground still as though it were dead. Just as Lisa began to panic, Cheyenne began rolling the puppy around with her nose. Then she began tossing it around quite roughly and the puppy sneezed and started breathing. Lisa cried as she witnessed this tiny miracle.

Cheyenne went on to deliver six puppies just as Lisa suspected. She vigorously cleaned each one as they were born and then settled down and nursed all of them together. Cheyenne was a great Mom already. Lisa was glad that she had witnessed four of the six puppies being born, and went back to bed.

Early the next morning, which was the morning of Christmas Eve, six hungry puppies crying to be fed woke up the boys. "Mom, Mom, Cheyenne had her puppies in our room!" Beau cried.

"Mom, Cheyenne had puppies in the boys' room! Six of them! I could hear them crying all the way in my room!" exclaimed Lindsay.

Jeff rolled over still half asleep and said, "You were right, honey; she had six sausages."

"She had four boys and two girls!" declared Lindsay.

It seemed as though Cheyenne was famous, judging by the number of visitors she had. There were even people knocking on the door whom they didn't know but who knew Cheyenne and wanted to get a peek at her puppies. Bagheera was also curious. He would walk as slowly as possible toward the puppies, only to have Cheyenne growl at him. It looked like it hurt his

feelings when she growled, because he would slowly lie down and put his big head in between his legs and just look at the pups from a distance. It didn't take long, however, for Cheyenne to figure out that Bagheera was not a threat to her babies. In fact, Bagheera quickly acquired the name Uncle Bagheera. He usually wanted to be in the house right next to the puppies, and when he lay down beside them, the pups would crawl in and around his legs and sometimes they would fall asleep right in between his big paws.

During the first few weeks, the puppies all looked the same. They actually looked like purebred dachshunds. But then it happened … scruff. The pups started growing scruff around their faces. By time the puppies were three weeks old, they all looked like mutts.

The arrival of puppies had been a learning experience for the whole family and very demanding timewise for everyone. Feeding, cleaning and caring for the puppies took a couple of hours each day. Jeff and Lisa decided that Cheyenne would never be allowed to have puppies again. Not even a purebred litter. It was just too much work. Lisa had worked hard to secure good homes for each puppy, a task that didn't come easy. Not everyone wants a dog—not even a small dog.

When the puppies were six weeks old, they were ready to go to their new homes. Their new owners would be coming over during the next day or two to pick them up. Lisa made birth certificates for the puppies and put blue collars on the boys and pink on the girls.

"Beau, can you please brush the puppies' fur so they look nice for their new homes?" Lisa asked, trying to occupy Beau while she was busy cleaning and Lindsay and Jeffrey were at school. Beau loved playing with the puppies, so he ran to get a brush. After Beau was quiet for what seemed like too long, his mom decided to check in on his progress. As Lisa walked into the kitchen, she saw fuzzy stuff all over the floor—brown and yellow fuzzy stuff. At first she didn't realize what it was, and then she knew. "Beau Justin Wright, what in the world have you done?"

Beau looked up at his mom and set her sewing scissors down on the floor. Lisa looked at the puppies and looked at Bagheera who seemed to be enjoying whatever it was that Beau was doing.

"My goodness, Beau, you gave them all a hair cut," exclaimed Lisa as she covered her mouth in shock. Bagheera and every one of the puppies had had their hair chopped up by Beau. There were even some places on them where it had been cut clear down to their skin and they were bald. It suddenly struck Lisa as hysterical, and she fought off the urge to laugh.

Lisa paused for a moment without saying a word. She looked at the pups, she looked at Bagheera, she looked at the mounds of fur all over the kitchen floor and then she looked at Beau's innocent face. "Well, Beau, I think that's plenty," Lisa said, realizing there was really no harm done. None of the dogs had been injured and they didn't seem to care about their haircuts at all. In time their hair would grow back to normal.

There was, however, some explaining to do to each person who came to get their pup. Lindsay and Jeffrey were more than happy to tell the story. "My little brother gave the puppies a haircut," said Lindsay to one person.

"He just did it yesterday, and he cut some all the way down to their skin," Jeffrey added. Everyone still took their puppy, and in the end everyone had a pretty good laugh.

Windsor Heights

Chapter 10

Riding Times Two

By February, it was time to make good on the promise to Lindsay. "Lindsay, I have been thinking; how would you feel about me taking lessons with you when you start back?" Lisa asked.

"I would like that. Why?"

"Well, you know that I want to ride, and I'm almost giving up on ever finding horse property. So the only way for me to ride would be to have lessons. There is only one catch," Lisa said.

"What's that?" Lindsay asked.

"If I ride with you, we will only be able to afford lessons every other week. If you ride by yourself, you can take lessons every week just like before," explained Lisa.

"I want you to ride with me, Mom," Lindsay said with a smile on her face.

"Are you sure you can handle the every other week thing?" Lisa asked, smiling too.

"Yes," Lindsay assured her mom.

"Then it's settled. I'll call Anne today and make arrangements for both of us to start lessons as soon as possible," declared Lisa.

"Mom, I'm warning you; you are going to be so sore when Anne gets done with you," Lindsay said laughing while she watched her mother dial.

"Shh!" signaled Lisa with one finger held up to her mouth. "Hello, Anne, it's Lisa ... Fine, thank you ... Lindsay and I would like to start back with you as soon as possible ... Yes, that's right, lessons for myself, too ... Do you have a horse that's big enough for me?" Lisa winked at Lindsay. "We will only be able to have lessons every other week ... Is that a problem for you? ... Great ... Okay, Anne ... Talk to you later ... Bye." Lisa hung up the phone.

"What did she say? Can she find a horse for you?" Lindsay spit out as fast as she could.

"Linds, settle down. She said she'll call us when she can line up two horses for us," Lisa said in a calm manner.

"Mom, you're going to need to get some boots and a helmet," Lindsay said excitedly.

"You're right. I forgot about that. Oh, great, now I have butterflies," Lisa said, rubbing her stomach.

After a few days, Anne called to let them know that she had found two horses that belonged to students of hers who were willing to let them be used in lessons. Lindsay would ride Noah and

Lisa would ride Gatlin. Their lessons would be held at a different stable in the same area.

"These boots feel funny. I hope the neighbors don't see me," Lisa said, adjusting her leggings under her boots.

"Mom, they look fine," Lindsay said assuredly.

Lisa stood up and took an overall look of herself in Lindsay's full-length mirror. Now rather proud of her new equestrian look, she said, "Actually, I hope the neighbors do see me."

"My toes are touching the end of my boots, Mom," Lindsay said.

"They are? Darn. I suppose you probably have outgrown them by now. Do you think you can get by with them today?" asked Lisa in concern.

"Yeah, I'll be fine. But we better go now," Lindsay said, daring not to spoil their first lesson. Lisa and Lindsay each grabbed their helmets and headed out the door.

Driving to their lesson, Lisa began to reminisce, "I really can't believe I'm going to have an English lesson. When I used to trail-ride with my friends, we liked to ride by the 4-H arena when they had shows to see all the fancy show horses and snooty English riders. Then we would make fun of them all the way home. We would stick our rears out, posting up and down and stick our noses up in the air to look like snobs. We would end up laughing so hard that we nearly fell off our horses. Oh, those were fun times." Lisa laughed which made Lindsay laugh. Lindsay liked to hear her mom tell stories of when she was little.

"Mom, tell me the story of when you made Annie put mud on Snowball," Lindsay requested.

Lisa began laughing just thinking of it. "Well, one day just after it had rained, Annie and I rode down to the old 'Bob and Jeans' restaurant. We tied Indian and Snowball up to the hitching post where they had to stand in nearly a foot of mud and then went inside to have lunch. We were having a great time eating when suddenly all the people in the place started laughing hysterically while looking out of the window. It was hard to hear what people were saying through all the laughter, but what Annie and I gathered, was that it had something to do with someone's horse rolling in the mud. Somehow I knew it was my horse, so Annie and I went outside to check on our horses. Sure enough it was Indian down rolling in the mud looking more like a pig in a pigpen. My pad was a muddy mess and Annie was laughing hysterically."

Lindsay began to laugh. "And then what, Mom?"

"Well, I took one look at little pure, white Snowball and told Annie that it was only fair for her to put some mud on Snowball, too."

"Oh, gosh, Mom!" Lindsay said giggling. "I can't believe you said that."

"So I guess Annie felt sorry for me," Lisa said, continuing the story, "So she tromped through the mud and began taking handfuls of it and smearing it all over poor Snowball." Lindsay began laughing so hard that she had to hold her side.

"Poor Snowball, Mom."

"Anyway, that's when Annie got her foot stuck in the mud. And when she pulled her foot out she had lost a shoe. Now I was laughing uncontrollably while Annie was reaching around in the mud looking for her lost shoe. Once she pulled her shoe out, she decided that it was too muddy to put on, so she left it there. Then we both got on our muddy horses and rode them home laughing all the way. I can still see Annie now riding home with one muddy shoe and one muddy sock. That was a day that I will never forget."

"Mom, that was so mean of you," Lindsay said still laughing.

"I know, Lindsay, it sure was, but I guess it's true when they say, 'misery loves company.'"

Lisa and Lindsay were almost at the stables now. "It feels good to come up in this area again and smell the orange blossoms, doesn't it?" Lisa commented.

"Yeah, it does," Lindsay said.

"Hey, perfect timing," Lisa said, pulling up right behind Anne the trainer as they entered the gate of the new stable.

"Hi, guys!" called Anne, getting out of her van with a smile gleaming across her face. "How are you, Lindsay? I haven't seen you in a long time. Gee, I think your last lesson must have been seven or eight months ago," Anne said, looking at Lindsay.

"Anne, am I really riding Noah?" asked Lindsay.

"You sure are, sweetie," confirmed Anne.

"I remember him. We were in a lesson together when I was riding Fresno," Lindsay said, never forgetting a horses or detail.

"You're probably right," Anne said. "Well, let's not waste time; we'll need all the light we can get because there are no lights in the tack room and we only have an hour of daylight left. I need to show both of you where the owners of the horses you will be riding keep their saddles and bridles. They said you're welcome to use their tack, but, believe me, they're both very picky, so you need to make sure you put it back exactly the way you found it," Anne explained. Anne opened up the tack door and gave Lindsay a saddle and bridle. "This is for Noah," she said. Then she handed Lisa her saddle and bridle, saying, "And this is Gatlin's stuff. Can you manage to tack up on your own while I give Lindsay a hand?" asked Anne as she walked off before Lisa could even answer. Lisa stood there looking at the saddle she would soon be riding in. She took a deep breath and walked over to Gatlin.

"Hi, Gatlin. Do you mind if I ride you today?" Lisa asked as she opened the gate and haltered the big bay gelding.

Anne yelled from the other side of the stable, "We are almost done over here; I hope you are almost ready, too!" Lisa hurried and put the saddle and bridle on Gatlin and led him out of his corral. "Go ahead and get on," Anne said. Lisa tried to get her foot in the stirrup.

"I don't know, Anne," Lisa said in an uncertain voice. "This feels so strange. Maybe I should ride with a pad since that's what I'm used to."

"You'll be fine. Just take him over to the hay bales and you can get up easier from there," Anne said.

Lindsay watched confidently from Noah's back. "Go on, Mom, it's easy."

"I know, I know. I'm just not used to this," Lisa said, lining Gatlin up next to a bale of hay. Lisa got up on the bale of hay and threw her long leg over the horse and perched herself right up in the saddle. "Oh, this feels weird. Anne, I'm scared. I'm afraid my feet will get stuck in the stirrups."

Anne chuckled and put Lisa's feet in the stirrups for her. "There, now turn him around and walk him out to the arena. You'll be fine. Heels down both of you," Anne shouted.

Lindsay immediately spiked her heels straight down. Lisa tried, but her heels remained level.

"Lisa dear, you need to seriously get your heels down," Anne said. Lisa tried again.

"Do they look down now? They feel down."

"No, they are not down. I'll give you some exercises to do at home that will stretch out your calf muscles so it's easier for you next time. It does take time, but pretty soon it will feel completely natural," Anne told Lisa. "Lindsay, you look good," commented Anne, "Isn't Noah nice!"

"Yeah, he is," agreed Lindsay.

Anne began moving poles and cones around the arena, "There!" Anne said to herself, then brushed off her hands and smiled at Lisa and Lindsay, saying, "Okay, now both of you pick up your reins and begin to trot." Lindsay took off in a smooth consistent trot. "Good for you, Lindsay, you haven't missed a beat," Anne said. Lisa followed Lindsay as though it was no problem but soon found herself off-balance and bouncing all over the place. Anne let out an obnoxious laugh, "Stop! Just stop."

Lisa pulled Gatlin back and managed to stop him. Lisa was out of breath. Anne walked over to her and said, "It's not as easy as it looks, is it? Take your feet out of the irons." Anne held Lisa's ankle down against the iron. "I think your legs are as long as mine," Anne said with a smile on her face. Then she put Lisa's feet back in the newly adjusted stirrup and said, "There, now try that." Anne gave Lisa directions to begin trotting again. Once again Lisa struggled to maintain balance and rhythm. "Up, down, up, down, there you go ... can you feel it? ... yes ... yes ... keep going," yelled Anne.

Lisa stopped. "My legs are burning up! Oh, that is hard! I'm out of shape!"

"Gatlin is out of shape, too. He's already soaked with sweat," noticed Anne. Anne had mercy on Lisa and allowed them to walk for a minute while she focused on Lindsay. "Lindsay dear, do you think you still remember how to canter?" Anne asked.

"Oh, yeah," assured Lindsay.

"Okay then, please take Noah around the cones that I have set up in a nice easy canter," directed Anne. Lindsay didn't hesitate to command a canter out of Noah. "Beautiful ... beautiful Lindsay ... okay now trot ... walk ... and halt. Lovely!" Anne looked at Lisa as if to say you're next.

"Oh, Anne, I don't know. I'm not used to this saddle thing yet," Lisa pleaded.

Anne insisted, "Please do exactly what Lindsay did on Noah. You can do it."

Lisa reluctantly walked Gatlin over by the

cones that were set up in a circle. "I am seriously scared, Anne."

"Please ask for the canter by pulling gently on the left rein and kicking with your right foot. You will be asking for Gatlin's left lead to balance you while you are traveling around the circle to the left," explained Anne. Lisa held her breath and did what Anne said. Gatlin began to run around the cones, while Lisa was doing everything she could to look as graceful as Lindsay. Anne wasted no time in using her loud voice, "Your arms, your arms, keep them quiet! They are flapping like chicken wings." Lindsay began to laugh at her Mom flapping her arms. Lisa pulled Gatlin to a stop.

"Anne, I just can't do any more today. I'm really wiped out," Lisa said, breathing heavily. Anne walked over to Lisa and gave her some pointers on how to position her leg.

"My gosh, both of you are sweating. I don't think Gatlin has been worked lately. That's enough for today," Anne said. "Walk out your horses and then put them away. I will see both of you in two weeks."

Lisa didn't take another step on the horse. She got off in the arena and walked ever so wobbly back to the barn. Lindsay rode Noah back to his stall, unfazed by the lesson. Lindsay laughed at the way her Mom was walking with her legs still in the shape of the horse's body.

"I seriously don't think it's funny, Lindsay."

Lindsay let herself down off Noah and realized that she too was a bit sore. She then began to laugh even harder, "Oh, my legs!"

Lisa and Lindsay got in the van just as the sun was setting. "Oh, the sky is so beautiful, Lindsay. Look at all the palm trees lining the pink and orange horizon. I had a friend who moved to Wisconsin for college, and she told me that one of the things she really missed about home were the palm trees. You just don't see palm trees the way you see them in California, especially here in Riverside. Ever since she told me that, I have looked at palm trees differently and appreciated them more. Linds, squint your eyes, squint your eyes while you look at a palm tree."

Lindsay squinted her eyes like her Mom and looked out the window fixing her eyes on a palm tree. "Doesn't it kind of look like a firework? You know, the way they explode in the sky and then gracefully fall down?"

"Yeah, it really does," agreed Lindsay.

"I guess it will be a nice day tomorrow," Lisa said while driving toward home.

"How do you know, Mom?"

"Remember that saying, 'Red sky at night, sailors delight; red sky in morning, sailors warning.'"

"Oh, yeah, I remember that now."

Lisa stopped the van and rolled down her window. "What are you looking at, Mom?"

"Look at that sign, Lindsay." There was a big hand-painted sign on a piece of property

with weeds growing up all around it. The sign read, "For Sale by owner," with a phone number at the bottom of the sign slightly hidden by the tops of the weeds. "I guess that's the house way back there," Lisa said, pointing to a single-story house set very, very far back off the road. It was somewhat hidden behind very tall weeds and a huge overgrown elm tree. "Look at the driveway; it must be as long as two football fields put together. Gosh, and there's an orange grove along the whole side of the property. Lindsay, wouldn't that be neat to live right next to an orange grove?" Lisa said in awe.

"Yes, Mom, now can we please go? I have to go to the bathroom," Lindsay said impatiently. Lisa rummaged through the items on the floorboard of the van and found a pen.

"Just out of curiosity," Lisa said to herself as she wrote down the phone number and then slowly continued home while listening to Lindsay go on about how sweet Noah was.

Chapter 11

An Old House

Lisa couldn't wait to call the phone number on the sign she had seen. And when she did, she was surprised that there might actually be a chance they could afford the house. She set up a time for the whole family to have a look at the property.

When they arrived to view the house, they parked under the giant elm tree in front. Before they walked up to the door, Lisa had a few words with the children, "Please be quiet in their house, wipe your feet on the door mat, keep your hands to yourself and don't touch anything.

Do you understand?" Lindsay, Jeffrey and Beau nodded in unison.

They rang the doorbell, and soon an elderly couple opened the door and welcomed them in. The old lady did not waste a minute showing them the house. "I'll show you the back bedrooms first," she said as she began walking them down the hallway. There were three average-size bedrooms and one just slightly larger, which was the master bedroom. The ceilings were a standard eight feet high, unlike the high vaulted ceilings in the house they lived in.

"Mom, these roofs are low," Jeffrey said. Lisa put one finger over her mouth signaling for Jeffrey to keep quiet.

Lindsay couldn't resist the urge to speak. "We have blue carpet too," she told the old lady. After they had looked at the bedrooms, the lady walked them back through the house to the living room, which was where they had first come in. "This is a nice room for company," she said.

"Honey, look, a built-in book shelf," Lisa said.

"Yeah, it is nice," agreed Jeff. Then he caught a glimpse of the fireplace and exclaimed, "Now that's what I call a fireplace." There was a big brick fireplace that was four feet wide instead of two feet wide like the one they had.

"That fireplace is wonderful. It heats up this half of the house," the old lady said. From the living room, she proceeded to walk them into the kitchen. The kitchen was long and could be walked through from either side. It had an old sink with an old faucet that came out of the wall.

"Oh, how cute," Lisa said as she turned on the faucet and watched the water come out. The old lady then walked them into the kitchen eating and dining area where the old man was sitting drinking a cup of coffee. It was one space, but they had one side made fancy for dining and one side more casual for the kitchen eating area.

"We just put these wood floors in last year," she said, directing their attention to the floors.

"There you go, honey. You always did like wood floors," Jeff said to Lisa.

"Yes, I do love these floors," agreed Lisa. "Oh my gosh, look, honey, I have seen those in magazines," Lisa said as she stood admiring another fireplace set in a wall of bricks.

"That fireplace keeps the whole kitchen eating area warm," the old man said. Then he asked his wife, "Did you show them the pot-belly stove?"

"Not yet, dear," she answered. Then focusing on the children, asked, "Would you like to see downstairs?" Lindsay, Jeffrey and Beau looked at each other and smiled. They had always wanted to live in a house with stairs. The old lady walked them into the next room, which had just two steps to walk down.

Lisa pointed to the stairs and smiled, "Hey kids, it *is* a two-story house."

"This is our family room and where we spend most of our time. We watch TV, read and even eat on trays down here, and when the pot-belly stove is burning, it gets nice and toasty in here," the old lady said. The family room also had wood floors and big windows all around it with a view in front and in back of the house.

"Sweetie, let's show them the sun room," the old man said to his wife. The old lady walked them back up the two stairs, through the kitchen eating area, through a sliding glass door, and into a very long room with at least twenty windows that looked out to the back yard. The floor was tiled with big red Mexican tiles. The old man proudly told the story of when he took his old truck to Mexico and brought back the tiles that he tiled the floor with.

"This room is refreshing because it makes you feel like you're outside," the lady said.

The old man noticed that the children had their noses pressed up against the windows gazing at the big pool and jacuzzi in the back yard. He told the children, "The pool is shallow at both ends and deep in the middle."

After the whole house had been looked at, the old lady had the children sit down at the table. She placed a plate of homemade cookies in front of them and poured them each a glass of milk. Lindsay, Jeffrey and Beau looked at their mom and dad for permission to eat. "Go ahead, guys," Jeff said.

"I guess you would call this a ranch-style house," the old lady said. "It was built forty years ago, and we have lived here the last ten. It's just too much for us to take care of now."

The old man said, "We have had it for sale before and changed our minds, but the time has come for us to move on and downsize."

Lindsay, Jeffrey and Beau had barely said a word and were still eating cookies when their very overweight dog walked in the kitchen.

Beau blurted out, "I didn't know you had a fat dog. Can I pet him?"

Jeff shot Lisa a look as if to ask, "Did Beau really just say that?"

The old lady just laughed and said, "Oh, that's Zeke; she's a girl. Sure you can pet her."

"I would like to show you the rest of the property and the barn," the old man said.

"That would be great; we would like to see it," Jeff said. Lindsay, Jeffrey and Beau quickly swallowed down their last gulp of milk so they could see the property, too.

The old man led the way up the hill to the top of the property. "On a clear day, you can see for miles up here," the old man said, huffing and puffing, "Well, there is the barn, but I don't have a key for it right now. We just use it for storage."

"Where is the arena?" Lisa asked.

The old man, still breathing hard, pointed to what looked like weeds. "It's right there, but you can't see it right now due to the weeds. See the cables? It's right there. The people who built the house built the arena."

As Lisa walked closer, she finally saw it, "Oh, now I see it." There were old railroad ties leaning this way and that way with cables running through them to connect them. There were even some places that had barbed wire connecting them. Lindsay, Jeffrey and Beau had even found an old, old rusty swing set that they helped themselves to. Lisa walked over to the children and tried to speak under her breath, "You guys, get off that rusty old thing. It's probably forty years old and looks like it's going to break any second."

The kids got off the swing set, and they all walked down to where they had parked the van. Jeff shook the old man's hand, saying, "Thank you very much, sir, for showing us your place. Let us give it some thought and we will call you back."

"That sounds fine. And thanks for coming," the old man said. On their way home, Jeff and Lisa talked about the house. "So what do you think, honey?" Jeff asked Lisa.

"I really liked it. It's a simple house which is nice. But ten acres? Isn't that a lot to take care of?"

"No way, not if you have a tractor," Jeff said enthusiastically.

"So you liked it too?" Lisa asked.

"I don't think you'll ever find anything like it for the price they're asking, and it's only going to increase in value."

"So what are you saying?" Lisa asked.

"I think we should do everything we can to buy that house," Jeff said in a no-nonsense tone. "It's the only property we have seen that we could possibly afford. I don't mind fixing up the place. There's enough land to build a new barn some day if we wanted to. You could do anything you wanted to with that much land."

"Are we moving?" Jeffrey asked.

Lisa responded with a conservative answer, "Jeffrey, we don't know yet. We'll tell you if we are."

"I want the pink bedroom," Lindsay blurted out as fast as she could.

Jeffrey and Beau followed suit. "I want the green room," Beau said.

Jeffrey said, "I want the office with the cuckoo clock."

"Jeffrey, if we buy the house, they will take all their things with them. They won't leave the clock," Lisa corrected.

"I still want the office," Jeffrey insisted.

"Well, if we move, you boys will still share a room because you only have one bed."

"Oh, yeah," Jeffrey said. Beau looked relieved. He had always shared a room with his big brother and liked it that way. Beau couldn't even fall asleep without Jeffrey next to him in bed.

When they arrived home, Lisa became nostalgic about their quaint little house at the end of the road, "I do love this house, honey. I feel like I can take care of everything here, and the kids have their friends on the block to play with."

"I know you like it here now, but what

about in two years or five years when the kids are bigger? I think you'll be happy in that house. The kids will have each other to play with, and they will be closer because of it. You and Lindsay can have horses, the boys can have motorcycles, not to mention it's a good investment," assured Jeff.

"I guess you're right. It probably would be good for our family," agreed Lisa.

Jeff and Lisa went back and had one more look at the house just to make sure they really wanted to live there. Then, after much thought, they signed the papers to buy the house. They would move in June when the kids got out of school. Two weeks later while Lisa and Lindsay were on their way to their second riding lesson, Lisa drove by the house that would soon be theirs. "There it is, Linds. There's our house ... almost," Lisa said pointing.

During their lesson, Lisa told Anne about the house down the street that they were buying.

Anne could not contain her enthusiasm. "Oh, I have always loved that house. I am so glad that a good family like yours will be moving in there." Then she added, "By the way, I can help you find some horses when you get settled. I know a lot of people, so do let me help you with that."

"I don't know exactly when we will get horses. I think we'll probably wait a year and clean up the property. There's a lot of junk and barbed wire that could be dangerous to a horse," responded Lisa.

"Well, let me know," Anne said.

That night Jeff and Lisa began the ritual of tucking the kids in bed. Jeff tucked Lindsay in, and Lisa tucked the boys in. After all was quiet, Jeff told Lisa, "Lindsay told me that she is praying for a black horse."

"Midnight?" Lisa asked knowingly.

"Yeah. She really thinks she's going to get one, too," Jeff said.

"Let her wish," Lisa said. "There's nothing wrong with wishing and praying, is there?"

"I guess not," Jeff decided.

"Jeffrey told me that you were going to take him golfing on Mother's Day. Is that true?" Lisa asked.

"Your brother is planning a Mother's Day brunch at Coto de Caza Country Club. He said after brunch, the guys could golf nine holes and the girls could go to the stables and look at the horses," Jeff explained. "I told your brother that you might not like us golfing on Mother's Day."

"That's not exactly what I had in mind, but nine holes won't take that long, and it would be fun to walk through their stables," Lisa said.

Chapter 12

A Mother's Day Accident

"Happy Mother's Day," whispered Jeffrey to his mother who was still sleeping. Lisa opened her eyes and saw Jeffrey standing in front of her with a flower he had picked out of the yard. Beau was peeking around from behind his big brother so as not to get in trouble for waking his mom.

"Thank you, boys," Lisa said as she yawned. Now that she was awake, the boys started talking in a louder tone of voice.

"Mom, when I go golfing with Dad today, I'm going to wear my baseball hard hat just in case I get hit in the head with a golf ball," Jeffrey said.

"That's a good idea, Jeffrey," Lisa said as she got out of bed still yawning.

"Am I golfing, Mom?" asked Beau.

"I don't know. Did you ask Dad? Where is Dad anyway?" Lisa wondered.

"He's getting donuts to surprise you," Beau said.

Lisa smiled and gave Beau a hug, saying, "When are you going to learn to keep a secret?"

The kids heard the front door slam. "Dad's home!" they screeched as they raced into the kitchen to get the best donut.

"I get a sprinkle!" Jeffrey said.

"I get another sprinkle!" Lindsay said running out of her room.

"I get a mable!" Beau said. Lindsay and Jeffrey laughed.

"Beau, it's not called mable, it's called maple!" corrected Lindsay.

"Hey, wait a minute, settle down," Jeff told the children. "Mom gets the first pick." Jeff wrapped his arms around Lisa and gave her a kiss, "Happy Mother's Day. Did you guys tell Mom happy Mother's Day?"

Lindsay, Jeffrey and Beau gave their mother a hug. "Happy Mother's Day," they said at once and then waited for her to get the donut of her choice.

"They all look so good, but I think I will have a *mable* bar," Lisa said as she pulled a big maple bar out of the box and winked at Lindsay and Jeffrey. They all sat down at the kitchen table to eat their donuts.

"After you guys are finished eating, everyone needs to get ready to go to Orange County. It's about a 45-minute drive to Coto de Caza Country Club, and I want to leave early," said Jeff as he practiced his golf swing with no club in his hand. Lisa laughed. "I feel like a million bucks right now. Kids, I hate to say this, but I'm going to smoke your Uncle David on the fairways today," Jeff said still doing practice swings. The kids laughed.

"Dad, I want to go with you!" begged Lindsay.

"Mom is taking you and Beau to the stables to look at the horses while Jeffrey and I are golfing," Jeff said, confident that would satisfy her. Lindsay raised her eyebrows in delight.

Brunch at the country club was wonderful. The conversation around the table was light-hearted. "So, Lindsay, tell me about your riding lessons. I hear your mom is taking lessons with you now," Aunt Judy inquired.

"They're fine. I'm riding a horse called Noah. He's an Arabian," Lindsay answered.

"You guys are so lucky. That sounds like fun," Aunt Judy said.

There was more food than one could possibly eat, including a whole table of desserts. Lindsay,

Jeffrey and Beau along with their cousins Joseph and Luke made several trips to the dessert table.

When everyone was just about finished eating, Uncle David got up from the table and said, "So, big guy, are you ready for me to beat you on the greens?"

Jeff laughed. "Uncle David, my dad said that he was going to smoke you on the fairways today," Jeffrey said.

Uncle David looked at Jeffrey, "Is that what he said?" Then he looked at Jeff. "I don't know about that big guy; I am feeling pretty good today. Let's go, Jeffrey, come on Joseph."

"When we finish nine holes, we'll meet you at the stables. I'd say an hour and a half," Jeff told Lisa.

The stables were fun for the first hour and a half, but then after two hours, it was beginning to get boring. "I wonder where those guys are," Lisa said to Aunt Judy.

"I don't know. They should have been back by now," Aunt Judy said.

"Why don't we drive back to the country club and wait for them there," suggested Grandma.

Grandma drove back through Coto de Caza. As they passed the small fire station, Aunt Judy noticed Jeff's truck parked in the driveway with both doors swung wide open. There was also an ambulance and paramedics walking around. "Stop, Marian!" Judy yelled. Lisa saw the truck, she saw her brother and Joseph, and then she saw Jeff. Lisa noticed that Jeff had a terrible look on his face. Something had happened. Aunt Judy began to panic and yelled, "Where's Jeffrey, where's Jeffrey? Something is wrong!"

"Be quiet, Judy!" Lisa snapped as she assessed the situation. As soon as Grandma parked the car, Lisa jumped out, fearing something awful. Lisa ran up to Jeff, "Where's Jeffrey? Is he okay?"

"He's going to be alright," Jeff said. Lisa noticed that Jeff was dirty, he had dirt on his clothes, knees and arms, and he was limping. Lisa walked around the ambulance and saw Jeffrey belted down on a stretcher. Jeffrey started to cry at the sight of his mother. Lisa knelt down beside Jeffrey and held his hand.

"Are you Jeffrey's mother?" a paramedic asked Lisa.

"Yes, can someone please tell me what happened?" Lisa asked in a surprisingly calm yet serious manner.

"We won't know all the details without X-rays, but so far it appears as though he has broken his leg," the paramedic said.

Lisa hugged Jeffrey and ran her fingers through his curly blond hair, "You're going to be just fine, Jeffrey," Lisa said in a somewhat relieved tone.

"We need to get him to the hospital. You can ride in the ambulance with us if you like," the paramedic told Lisa.

"Of course," Lisa said. As they loaded Jeffrey in the ambulance, Lisa walked over to Judy, who was still in a state of hysteria, and said, "They think he broke his leg."

"No!" shouted Judy, "Oh, poor Jeffrey!"

Lisa turned to her brother, "David, how did this happen?"

"Jeffrey crashed the golf cart in the bottom of a ravine," he said. Before Lisa could respond, the paramedics motioned for her to get in.

While in the ambulance on their way to the hospital, the paramedic handed Lisa the baseball hard hat that Jeffrey had been wearing. It was cracked and scratched. "It's a good thing he was wearing a hard hat. From the looks of it, it probably saved his life," he said.

Later at the hospital, Jeff and Lisa waited with Jeffrey for hours in the emergency room until he was treated. Jeffrey had been given pain medication which allowed him to sleep. "Tell me exactly how this happened. David said that Jeffrey crashed in a ravine," Lisa said.

Jeff began to tell the story, "I was driving the

golf cart and Jeffrey kept asking if he could drive it. I knew it wasn't a good idea, but when I got out to make a putt on the green, I asked Jeffrey to pull the cart over closer. I thought he could do it." Jeff continued, "I wasn't even watching, but then I heard the golf clubs rattling in the back of the cart, and when I looked up, I saw Jeffrey headed for a cliff. I ran as fast as I could to stop him, but I couldn't catch him. Jeffrey screamed my name as the golf cart went down the side of the ravine. It hit a tree stump and Jeffrey was thrown out in front of the cart. The cart continued down the hill and pinned him at the bottom. That's when I took a flying leap over the edge and really hurt both of my knees getting to Jeffrey. I could see that the front bumper of the golf cart was right up against both of his thighs and he told me that his leg was broken. Then I grabbed the golf cart and somehow I threw it off of him. I knew I had to get him out of there, so I gently carried him up the steep hill and held him as your brother drove us in his golf cart back to my truck. I knew his leg was broken because I could feel it moving when I was holding him. I tried really hard to keep it still." Jeff sat quietly pondering the whole situation shaking his head in disbelief. "I don't think I will ever forget Jeffrey's scream for the rest of my life."

"I was actually relieved when the paramedic told me it was Jeffrey's leg they were concerned about. I was thinking that he might have been hit in the head with a golf ball or golf club and had brain trauma or something. But the minute I saw Jeffrey on that stretcher, and he looked at me, I wasn't worried. I knew that he would be okay," Lisa said.

"It's a miracle that he lived through it," Jeff said.

Later that night, Jeff's brother Scott walked into the room to see Jeffrey. Jeffrey was asleep and never knew that his Uncle Scott came to visit him. Scott stayed for a short while and somehow, through his lighthearted sense of humor, made

Jeff feel a little better. "Hey, accidents happen. Just remind me not to ride in a golf cart if Jeffrey is driving," Scott said. Then in a more serious tone, he asked, "Before I go, do you mind if I pray?" Scott walked to the bedside of Jeffrey and laid his hands on his broken leg, "Lord, we thank you for Jeffrey's life. We certainly don't know why things like this happen, but we know that you love us and that you love Jeffrey. We ask that you help Jeffrey to get through this and that he might have a quick recovery. Amen." Lisa began to cry.

Jeff shook his brother's hand and with his other hand grabbed his arm in kind of a half hug, and said, "Thanks for coming." Lisa gave Scott a hug goodbye.

It was after midnight before the orthopedic surgeon arrived. After studying the x-rays of Jeffrey's leg, he told Jeff and Lisa that Jeffrey had a floating knee. The doctor explained that a floating knee meant that Jeffrey's femur bone was broken above his knee and that also his fibula bone and tibia bone were broken below his knee. Lisa didn't know what all that really meant. She just wanted the doctor to fix him. "Well, how long will it take you to cast his leg?" Lisa asked the doctor and then added, "I would like to get him home. It's late."

The doctor looked at Lisa and said, "He's going to have to stay here."

"Oh, so he can go home tomorrow then?" asked Lisa.

The doctor looked at Jeff and then back at Lisa. "Jeffrey has a serious injury. He will go into surgery tonight and remain in traction here at the hospital for three to four weeks while his bones set straight. Then he will be able to go home with a new cast which he will have for another six weeks." Lisa didn't say a word. The doctor assured Jeff and Lisa that he would take very good care of Jeffrey.

Jeffrey was put in a traction device to hold

his leg straight while it healed. He remained in traction for three and a half weeks. Jeffrey couldn't move; the only thing he could do was pull up on a bar above his bed to help lift himself up when the nurses changed his sheets. At first Jeffrey hated having the sheets changed because it hurt to move. In fact, he didn't want anyone to even bump his bed because that made his leg hurt. But as time went on and his leg healed, he got very good at pulling himself up on the bar. The hospital became a second home, not only to Jeffrey, but also to Lindsay and Beau. Jeffrey was rarely alone there. Jeff would spend nights with Jeffrey, while Lisa and Beau would spend days with him. Beau would crawl right in bed with Jeffrey and watch cartoons with him. Lindsay came to the hospital after school and would do her homework there.

When the doctor finally gave orders that Jeffrey could go home, they put him in a brand

new blue cast. It came all the way up to his chest and went down not only his right leg, which was the one that was broken, but he was also cast half way down his left leg with a bar in the middle of his legs for stability. Jeffrey had to be wheeled around in a special reclining wheel chair because he could not sit up. When he did get home, he couldn't even fit down the hallway, so his bed had to be moved into the family room where the three children spent many hours playing and reading together.

Things changed during the period of Jeffrey being in his body cast. Lindsay and Beau became closer and played more than ever. Beau had a chance to act like a big brother by helping Jeffrey, and Lindsay learned another lesson in patience. Once again, all riding lessons would be canceled until Jeffrey made a full recovery.

Chapter 13

Moving Day

It had been a long three months since the Wright's first found the house they would soon be moving into. Lindsay and Beau were pushing Jeffrey outside in his wheelchair, waiting for their dad. Jeff told the children that he would be coming home with a truck big enough to put the whole house in. Granny was over helping Lisa pack up boxes. Lisa stopped what she was doing and gazed out the kitchen window. She saw Bagheera and Cheyenne lying in the front

lawn. Jeffrey had Kimba on his stomach petting her. Everything was peaceful, quiet.

"I hope we made the right decision," Lisa said.

Granny stopped what she was doing, "Oh, Lisa, you will be so happy. I think it's good for people to move once in a while anyway. You have already lived here eight years. And like you said, the kids shouldn't have too hard of a time adjusting since they are able to stay in the same school."

"Jeff said Kimba won't survive at the new house. I have a real hard time accepting that. I'm even worried about Cheyenne," Lisa said.

"Cats do have a hard time adjusting to new surroundings. You'll just have to keep an eye on both of them and not let them out at night," Granny said.

"I guess," Lisa said as she continued packing.

Honk! Honk! Jeff had pulled up in the

driveway in a huge stake-bed truck with Papa. Lindsay ran up to the door and waited for her dad to get out of the truck. "Dad, can I have a ride? Can I have a ride?"

Jeff picked Lindsay up and sat her in the driver's side of the big truck. Lindsay bounced up and down on the seat and pretended to be steering the big truck.

"I can't give you a ride right now, but after Papa and I pack up the truck, you can help us make the first trip to the new house if you want to," Jeff said. Beau just looked up at the truck and stayed close to Jeffrey.

Papa went over and picked up Beau, asking, "Do you want to get in the big truck?"

Beau shook his head no.

"Jeffrey, I sure wish I could put you up in that truck, but I don't think you would fit with your leg out the way it is," Papa said in a sympathetic voice.

"Honey, the first trip will be things that go

in the garage. I won't have the key to the house until later, when the realtor brings it by," Jeff informed Lisa.

In a short time, Jeff and Papa had the whole truck filled with things mostly out of the garage. Papa was tired and hot. He pulled up a chair and sat down right next to Jeffrey. Jeff kept up a steady brisk pace in and out of the garage, getting more and more things to stack on top of the already filled truck.

"Papa, is that stuff going to fall out on the road?" asked Jeffrey.

"I think your dad is going to tie everything down so that won't happen," Papa said.

When the truck was ready to leave, Jeff yelled for Lindsay, "Let's go, Lindsay!"

Lindsay was now busy riding her bike with her friends on the block. "Dad, can I stay home?"

Jeff waved at her and pulled out of the driveway.

Later that day, the realtor showed up with the keys to the new house. Lisa welcomed him into

their now almost vacant house. They chatted for a while and then, before he left, he pulled the keys out of his pocket and jingled them in front of Lisa. "This is the last thing I need to do. I hope you and your family will be very happy with your new home in Windsor Heights." Lisa held out her hand and accepted the keys.

"Windsor Heights?" Lisa said as if asking for an explanation.

"That's right," the realtor said chuckling, "no one knows that area is called Windsor Heights, but it's on the city map by that name."

Lisa waved goodbye to the realtor and stood with her back to the door and pondered for a moment. While looking down at the keys she was holding, Lisa began talking quietly to herself, "Windsor Heights ... we live in Windsor Heights."

Just then Jeff walked in and heard Lisa. "What are you talking about?" he asked with a funny look on his face.

Lisa laughed, "Oh, nothing, the realtor was just here and left the keys to the house. By the way, do you know the name of the area where we will be living?"

"No, I guess I don't," Jeff said.

"Windsor Heights," Lisa said in an aristocratic tone of voice.

Jeff laughed at Lisa, "Okay, enough games. Let's get the rest of the stuff packed up and get out of here."

Finally, every last thing was packed. Jeff and Lisa hoisted Jeffrey, wheel-chair and all into the van first. Then they hoisted Bagheera, who was now partially paralyzed in one of his back legs, into the van. Beau got in next holding Cheyenne, and Lindsay got in holding Kimba and shut the door.

"Is everyone in?" Lisa asked exasperated.

"Yes!" Lindsay, Jeffrey and Beau said together.

Lisa put her gearshift into drive and under her breath said, "Windsor Heights, here we come!"

The Windsor Heights Series

Windsor Heights

To The Country

Moon and Midnight

The Auction

The Great Gift

Sugar and Cheyenne

Dazzle

The Black Gelding

Windsor Heights Coloring Book, Volume I

Windsor Heights Coloring Book, Volume II

CPSIA information can be obtained
at www.ICGtesting.com
Printed in the USA
FSOW02n2245210917
38820FS